The Devil Wears A Choir Robe:

Lust Lies And Deceit

D1519800

Destiny

TEXT UCP TO 22828 TO SUBSCRIBE TO OUR
MAILING LIST
If you would like to join our team, submit the first 3-4
chapters of your completed manuscript to
Submissions@UrbanChapterspublications.com

To my love, Jim

Thank you for giving me that extra push. I needed it.

Chapter One
Honor Thy Mother

At five feet four, with creamy, brown skin, and a body to die for, Brishelle couldn't figure out why she was still not married. She had just turned thirty-two this past March and thought she would have at least been married by thirty. She'd been on countless bad dates, thanks to an online dating app called Matchr, and had yet to find "the one". By thirty-two, she expected to have her dream career, a couple of children, and a handsome man by her side while living in Los Angeles. Although L.A. was quite expensive, she was sure she could make it with the dual income that was necessary to even fathom buying a house in the City of Angels. However, the dual income was only granted to young women who were lucky enough to find a husband.

Brishelle was born and raised in Inglewood. She never wanted to move anywhere else, even though her friends said there were far more eligible bachelors in the South, like in Georgia. Dating was hard in L.A., but her career as the owner, writer, and editor of *HeyBlackGrl! Magazine* wouldn't be possible without all the connections she had made in the city.

Brishelle had landed her dream job working for herself two years ago. She used to work for an advertising agency that she somewhat loved, but hated meeting deadlines and writing only to meet the needs of picky clients. She didn't see a lot of room for creativity in the advertising business. She had always wanted to create an online publication to celebrate lifestyle, beauty, and romance for Black women by Black women.

She was usually overwhelmed with story ideas to add to her website that discussed healthy eating, exercise, and travel. However, her romance section was pretty dry, and she was looking for a new freelance writer to help her out in that area. Brishelle hadn't had much luck in the romance category, so she hated writing about it, but knew it was an important topic in most women's lives. Writing about date ideas and how to look for the perfect guy gave her anxiety. It always brought back the depressed thoughts she felt when she scrolled down her social media timeline only to see the happy faces of her newly married friends with their new babies. It seemed like all her white and Asian friends from college were married already. A few of her black girlfriends were, too, but the vast majority were single with kids.

Brishelle had an updated vision board in her Lemeirt Park apartment with her favorite wedding dress styles, men she found attractive, a gorgeous home, and black children with natural hair. She felt if she could envision this life, it would someday happen for her. Every night, she prayed that God would finally send her the man she needed to make her life complete. Her best friend, Tiera, said she had too many qualifications that no man would be able to meet. Brishelle wanted a man who was at least six feet tall, in shape, white teeth, God-fearing and attended church regularly, made at least $75,000 a year, didn't live with their mother, no criminal background, at least one college degree, and didn't have any children. Brishelle believed her qualifications for a husband were certainly within reason. That was why Tiera was always getting caught up with bums, she thought. She felt her best friend had no standards and would rather be with anybody with a penis than set some limits in her love life.

Brishelle had always been described as gorgeous by everyone she knew. She had DD cup breasts that sat nicely in the low necklines she liked to wear. She had no more than a twenty-six-inch waist that she worked hard for in the gym. She also had a smooth, chocolate complexion that her family said made her look like a living doll. She kept her nails done in some shade of pink, which was her favorite color. She believed that every woman should keep their nails and hair done at all times. She never left the house without makeup. What if she ran into someone she knew at the grocery store? To Brishelle, looks were everything, and she had that down. She had an apple booty that fit nicely in every pair of skinny jeans she owned. She didn't believe in wearing clothes that didn't fit her body like a glove. She was blessed with a beautiful figure, so why not flaunt it?

Brishelle's only thorn in her side at this moment was her mother, Linda. She was worried that her daughter might never get married. She had hoped to have at least one grandchild by the time Brishelle was thirty. Brishelle was her only daughter and was her only hope of participating in a wedding at this point. She was constantly trying to set Brishelle up on dates with nice young men she met while out and about or at large church functions. She was set on finding her daughter a "real man of God". She and her husband, Henry, had been married for thirty years, and she had Brishelle, her only child, when she was twenty-two. Brishelle was her princess, but she was sure it was Brishelle's fault that she still hadn't been able to find her prince. She thought her daughter was too picky and should start looking at men who had a good value system and had a great work ethic. Brishelle just wanted her mother to stay out of her love life.

"Momma! I'm good. I don't need your help locating my future husband. I got this." Brishelle was exasperated dealing with her mother's meddling when all she had come over for was to check in with the dogs she had left with them when she moved out about ten years ago.

"I'm comfortable with being single right now, momma. I'm not dating heavy like I used to."

"Now you know that's a lie," her mother sneered. "I birthed you in this world, and I know when my child needs companionship. You out there in the middle of the city, tryna make it on your own. Even God said it isn't good for man to be alone."

"Exactly, momma. MAN to be alone!"

"Don't sass me, gal! You know what I meant. I'm just trying to help you out because since I been leaving it up to you, you still single."

The two stared at each other in the middle of the living room like two lions in the jungle. Her mother, being the bigger lion, wasn't backing down.

"Momma! I don't need you all up in my life like this. I'm a grown-ass woman, and I know what I need. Just because you've been married to Daddy for thirty years doesn't mean that's how I'm gonna end up, and I really don't care at this point."

"Oh, you do too care! You just saying that because your standards are sky high. Even Jesus couldn't meet 'em!"

"Wow, OK. I'm done talking to you for the day. I have to get back to work."

At this point, Brishelle wanted to burst into tears, but she didn't want to let her mother know how bad her words had hurt her. She definitely desired a husband and children one day, and it pained her that none of this had worked out by the time she reached thirty. She was starting to think that maybe something was wrong with her, and maybe she wasn't as beautiful or as sexy as she thought.

"Now the bible says to honor thy mother and thy father that thy days—" her mother blurted.

"I'm leaving, momma! I'll talk to you later!"

Brishelle walked swiftly to the door and unlocked it. She ran back to her car, a shiny, black Jetta, with tears in her eyes. She could barely see where she was going. Once she was in the car, she burst into a flood of tears while backing out of the driveway. She drove unusually fast to get back home. She was so upset with her mother. Why did she always remind her of how single she was? Why couldn't she just stay out of her life as asked?

She planned to try and distance herself from her mother but knew that wouldn't work because her mother was extremely anxious, and would report her missing if Brishelle even tried to ignore her for a few days.

Brishelle decided to turn off her phone for a few hours. She wanted to be alone. She decided to take her list of qualifications for a husband out of her journal again and cross out some of the unnecessary items. *Does he really need to make at least $75,000? Can he be 5'11?*

How much would she have to compromise to find the one?

Chapter Two
Single and Looking

On a dreary Sunday morning, Brishelle was wide awake but still in bed. Her headscarf had slipped off in the middle of the night, so her freshly done weave was strewn all over her pillow. She had even forgotten to wipe her makeup off last night because she had cried herself to sleep. The husband qualifications list was torn into pieces on the floor. She felt like giving up her search for some man to complete her life. Maybe her mother was right.

All of a sudden, Brishelle's phone lit up unexpectedly.

It was her mother calling at eight a.m.

She didn't want to pick it up, but she promised herself that she wouldn't stay on the phone longer than five minutes by giving her some lame excuse. She had to get started on placing more ads on the website today anyway.

"Hello? Momma, it's eight a.m. I'm barely up," she said in a dry, throaty voice.

"You need to start coming to the house of the Lord more often. Come and go to church with me today."

"Momma, I'm busy today. I have a lot of work things to do."

"Too busy for the Lord?" her mother retorted.

Brishelle sighed. She didn't feel like arguing about church this morning. Fortunately, she had recently decided to strengthen her relationship with God and had planned on going to church soon, just not this particular Sunday.

"Just come on and get dressed. I can come and get you."

"That's OK, momma. I can drive. I might want to leave a little early, and I know you like to stay," Brishelle said weakly.

"Well, praise God! I'll see you at eleven!"

"Wait, momma! Is it the church we used to go to?" Brishelle said, trying not to roll her eyes too hard.

"Glory Harvest Church of God in Christ over there on Berring Street."

"The pastor is Bishop—"

"I got it, momma. I'll see you then. Bye!"

"Bye, Breezy."

Brishelle hated being called Breezy, but she had recently learned to embrace it.

Still feeling groggy from staying up so late, Brishelle decided to crawl out of her bed and find some dressy clothes for church. She hadn't been to church in a long time, so she didn't have many dresses that were appropriate enough for an event outside of clubbing. She decided to wear a black pleated skirt that almost came down to her knees, a white blouse, a cheap rhinestone necklace that she had bought at a flea market, patent leather pumps, and her black Chanel clutch that she used only on special occasions.

Brishelle had hated getting dressed up for church for as long as she could remember. It seemed like no matter what she wore, it was never conservative enough for the Lord's house, according to her mother. She remembered being told to cover her arms with a shawl and to wear itchy pantyhose in the middle of the hot summer.

Brishelle put on red matte lipstick and sprayed some of her best perfume that she only wore when going on dates or to a networking event. She knew her mother was going to try and push one of those strange looking churchmen to ask her out on a date, but she decided to look good anyway, just in case someone was there who might catch her eye.

She poured a cup of coffee, turned on some boring Sunday morning news program, and ate wheat toast while her curling iron warmed up.

Her curls hadn't come out exactly as she had wanted, but it was almost 10:45, and she'd have to start heading out.

What you up to today?

Her friend Tiera's text lit up on the screen of her phone.

Headed to church. Brishelle quickly texted back as she gulped down her now-warm coffee because it had taken too long to curl her hair.

Oh really? Tryna get saved, huh?

Girl, shut up! I'm 'bout to leave now. I'll text you later. Brishelle turned her phone on vibrate and headed out the door.

She pulled up to the church's parking lot, and it was already full. She assumed these were all the people who had come early for Sunday school. She always hated going to Sunday school when she was growing up. It was a time for church members to argue about the most minor verses in the bible to seem smarter and holier than everyone else.

As she exited her car, a church mother who she remembered when she was a little girl, ran over to hug her.

"Brishelle! Now I ain't seen you in a *long* time!" the older woman, who seemed like she was sweating bricks by just existing, shouted.

"Oh, hi…yeah, how are you?" Brishelle stammered.

"You coming to service today?"

"Yes, I was gonna stay."

"Well, praise God! Your momma already in there!"

The older woman seemed a little "off," but nice. Church people were always a little "different," but she had gotten used to it.

"Yes, I know. Thank you. It was nice meeting you."

Brishelle quickly stepped away so she could find a seat away from everybody. She wanted to sit towards the back, but her mother motioned for her to come sit next to her. Brishelle tried not to roll her eyes and smile through it. She hated sitting towards the front because everyone would be looking at her. Sitting in the front made yourself a target during offering when everyone got up and made a beeline toward you to ask personal questions while you were trying to put your checkbook away.

Promptly at eleven a.m., the morning service started with the praise team singing all the praise songs Brishelle had grown up on. She knew all the words and stood up from time to time when they sang one she knew.

> *Oh God's got a way that you can't go under!*
> *God's got a way that you can go 'round it!*
> *God's got a way that you can't go over!*
> *You must come in at the door!*

The praise team consisted of two older women and two younger, attractive women harmonizing. She assumed that they were all part of the choir as well. Although their voices filled up the room, it still seemed like it was missing something. There were only the bass guitarist and the drummer playing.

The pastor hadn't arrived yet, and people were still walking in, trying to get their seat. Growing up, she remembered church members having unofficial assigned seats. No one could sit in the front, right corner except Mother Brown, and the very back corner of the church was reserved for somebody's prodigal son who was in and out of jail and had half the girls in the neighborhood pregnant at the same time.

It didn't seem as if the usher had to escort anyone to their seat because it seemed as if everyone knew where to go. Everyone seemed to know each other, too, so that meant she was going to get stares all morning long. She could feel people trying to size her up behind her back. They were probably wondering where she had come from, why she wasn't wearing pantyhose, and where her man was.

Brishelle instinctively knew to ignore church people, but couldn't help turning behind her and smiling every ten minutes or so, just to let people know she wasn't stuck up, and if her mother had never motioned towards her, she'd be sitting in the back.

Suddenly, almost everyone stood up with the praise team, singing a string of congregational songs that all sounded alike, but with different lyrics.

Then, a tall, chocolate man of about 6'3 walked in from the side door of the church and swooped in to turn on the keyboard. He began to catch up with the singers. He knew exactly which key they were in and didn't have to guess. He was so brilliant. He played like a Black Beethoven for Gospel music. His fingers seemed to glide over the keys like water. He didn't even have to look down at his hands. He was focused on the singers and smiling with them.

Brishelle's heart started to flutter like butterflies escaping from the wind.

He was so damn fine.

They still have men who look like that in the church? Brishelle thought.

His complexion was smooth like a chocolate candy bar. There wasn't a blemish anywhere to be found, except those two deep dimples on either side of his face.

He had straight, white teeth that were almost too perfect to be human. *He must not drink coffee or even eat,* she thought.

He reminded her of one of her favorite actors, like Morris Chestnut or Shaft from those seventies movies.

His eyes were deep, dark, and mysterious. They were focused on the praise team and the other musicians. He would look back at the drummer and laugh when they would start a song on a different rhythm. He seemed to be having the time of his life playing that keyboard, and Brishelle was having the time of her life watching him.

She tried not to stare at him so she wouldn't look too obvious, but she couldn't help herself. He was too beautiful for words. All she wanted to know was his name and if he was single.

Brishelle kept chanting in her head, *Please be single! Please be single!*

She hoped her brand new Victoria's Secret panties were still dry because she knew she wasn't supposed to be having unclean thoughts in God's house. But why would God tempt her with that fine specimen of a man right in front of her? Clearly, God said He would never tempt man, right? But Jesus was tempted by the devil, so to Brishelle, it wasn't such a far-fetched idea.

The pastor finally walked in, so Brishelle temporarily took her eyes off the keyboardist. The pastor seemed to be a man of about seventy who still walked around as briskly as a twenty-five-year-old. He was a balding, brown-skinned man wearing a black, tailored suit and a silver tie. He was about six feet tall, and those definitely weren't his teeth, but he seemed like a sweet man. His wife sat in the first row with a dark-blue church suit on that was typical of older church ladies. She had on a matching dark-blue hat that was tilted to the side. She was somewhat heavyset and seemed to smile at everyone who passed by her row. She appeared to be friendly, but Brishelle knew you could never totally trust church people. A heavenly smile could hide the most demonic jealousy.

His name was Bishop Michael A. Loving Sr., and the entire church stood up when he walked in, except the musicians. The keyboard player produced a beautiful intro as if the Queen of England had just entered the building.

"All right, church, you may be seated!" The pastor's voice boomed through the rows as if the church had surround sound, but he wasn't even using a microphone.

"Now, y'all ready to have some church? Gimme some more of that music, AJ!"

The pastor pointed towards the keyboardist.

AJ.

He had a name.

Brishelle had not only gotten to witness the embodiment of perfection, but perfection also had a name. AJ.

She wondered what AJ stood for, but she didn't care because at least she had something to call him if they ever happened to brush by each other. She couldn't wait until service was over so she could take advantage of the fellowshipping. She always hated shaking people's sweaty hands at the end of service, but she wouldn't mind shaking his. She was sure he had those big hands she loved. The ones that could grab you around your waist and almost go all the way around.

During prayer, she closed her eyes and began to ask God to send her a man just like AJ. As a matter of fact, she wanted to be sent AJ because he was everything she had always wanted in a man, and he had yet to open his mouth. He had a low-cut fade, eyes dark as sable, and broad shoulders that looked like he could protect her from a grizzly bear.

During the tithes and offering segment of the service, Brishelle took out the black Chanel wallet that matched her bag. She didn't have any cash, so she decided to write a check. The ushers directed half of the church around the altar, row by row. Brishelle noticed that each row had to march past the musicians. The keyboard player, AJ, was seated about five feet away from the first row in front of the altar where the pastor and assistant pastor sat. That meant she would have her chance to get a better look at him, and hopefully, get some eye contact.

As soon as the usher stood Brishelle's side of the church up, she mentally practiced how she would walk next to him without making her crush on him too obvious.

Brishelle walked along with the other church members to drop their envelopes in the gold collection pan. The choir sang harmoniously behind a woman, the lead soprano, who led the powerful but lively song.

When I think of his mercy and his kindness!
All I want to do is praise him!

AJ seemed to know the song well and kept his eyes on the audience rather than the choir.

Brishelle walked by and smiled.

He locked eyes with her and smiled back, nodding as if to say, "Welcome."

She could have fainted under the holy spirit right then and there after looking into his eyes. It was only for a second, but it felt like an eternity. She gave her biggest smile and nodded right back. She walked by with her sexy but classy switch. She had inherited her mother's wide hips and big booty that almost stuck out like a tabletop. Although she had a pleated, loose skirt, it was still possible to tell that she had more curves than a racetrack.

Brishelle dropped her envelope in the basket and walked back to her seat, following her row.
She sat next to her mother again, who was standing up, singing along with the choir.

Brishelle couldn't understand how her mother got so lost in the music. Although she hadn't been to church in a while, they still sang the same old songs she remembered. She was sure that Gospel artists had written and recorded some new ones by now. You would think that her mother would be bored, but she took in every song as if it were the first time she had ever heard it. Her mother tended to cry and shout every Sunday. It used to embarrass her when she was a little girl, but now she had gotten used to her mother veering towards the aisle to "cut a step" as they say.

Brishelle had never shouted before, but she wouldn't mind using it as an excuse to put herself out there in front of AJ. However, her mother would be able to see right through her. She would never get away with it, and might even be accused of "dancing out of the spirit," which meant that you "pretend" to dance for the Lord for attention.

Before Bishop Loving began his message for the morning, he decided to have someone sing a solo. Brishelle hoped he wouldn't preach for more than twenty minutes. Bishop Loving was known to be long-winded.

She decided to stay for the whole service for two reasons. She was sitting too close to the front and would make a scene, and she still wanted to see if she could at least greet AJ for a little bit after church.

The pastor grabbed both sides of the pulpit and swiftly pointed right at AJ.

"AJ! Gon' let your wife give me an 'A' selection!"

Wife?

Brishelle was floored. She should have known that someone that fine and perfect was taken. She wanted to storm out of the church but was more curious to see what this wife of his looked like.

One of the choir members stood up and motioned towards the mic stand. She was an overweight, light-skinned woman with long box braids. She had huge false lashes and bright purple lipstick. Even in a choir robe, Brishelle could tell she wasn't in very good shape. She didn't have a pleasant look about her, either. She seemed arrogant. It was as if she had been crowned "Best Singer in the Choir" and had run with it.

The woman sang a slow but beautiful rendition of "His Eye Is on the Sparrow".

After she sang, she smiled at her husband as he played a flowery ending to the song to lead into the pastor's message.

Brishelle knew she shouldn't still want this man, but she was very jealous. How did some women find such good men while successful women like her were still single? The wife wasn't very pretty and didn't seem that educated to her. She wondered what he would want with someone like her. She thought that maybe they were high school sweethearts and had just stayed with each other. She wondered if they had any children.

Brishelle looked around the church to see if there were any other eligible men who might be single. They were either old, too feminine, or had crazy eyes. A couple of the men looked like they might be ex-cons, but overall, there weren't that many men in the church in the first place, and that fat lead singer had taken the finest, most qualified one.

After church, Brishelle decided to go straight to her car. Her mother called her over before she could make it out of the door.

"Brishelle! Come here!"

Brishelle turned around and noticed her mother standing next to Morris Chestnut's twin aka AJ aka the married keyboard player.

She would look rude if she walked away, and she would look too eager if she ran over there, so she pretended to walk very slowly while shaking some of the church members' hands. An older man with breath that smelled like death on a stick stopped her and wanted to ask if she could join the outreach ministry. She said she would think about it and quickly turned away as if she had somewhere else to bring her attention to.

She stood right next to her mother, who was still talking to AJ.

"AJ, I want you to meet my daughter, Brishelle. Now she has a voice! I was wondering if you were looking for any more choir members."

"Oh, momma, no," Brishelle snapped.

"Oh, momma, yes! We're always looking!" AJ chuckled.

He seemed to even have a gorgeous personality to go with that face.

"Come by rehearsal this Thursday night around eight," he said with a wide smile.

"I'll have to see about my schedule. I tend to work late."

"Well, you can always make time to sing for the Lord," her mother interrupted.

Brishelle tried not to roll her eyes.

He reached out his hand to shake hers.

Brishelle was lost in his dark eyes and wanted to jump on him right then and there. She had never felt so sexually attracted to someone before. His married status had squelched some of those feelings earlier in the service, but being just a few inches away from him, she could almost smell his cologne. It smelled like Gucci by Gucci. Her ex used to wear that scent.

She shook his hand. It wasn't too dry or too soft. Just perfect.

She wanted to push him onto the nearest church pew and straddle him, but basic human decency kept her from embarrassing herself.

She knew she was wrong in the sight of the Lord for lusting after a married man. She promised that she would eventually stop thinking about him, but she also thought that joining the choir wouldn't be such a bad idea. She was an unofficial member of the church since she had been christened as a baby there and had stopped going sometime during college. She was always told she had a beautiful voice, so why not put it to practice? Singing was also her way of releasing stress and being creative. She promised she wouldn't join the choir to look at him. He was married anyway. She would join so she could begin to restart her life as a saved Christian woman, dedicating her life to God.

After they shook hands, they smiled at each other once again. He nodded and proceeded to break down the keyboard for the day so it could fit behind the organ.

Brishelle darted back home, playing loud Gospel music in the car. All of a sudden, the same sadness that she felt when she found out AJ was married came over her and tears started to stream down her face. She couldn't figure out why men like him always skipped over her and married other people. Even her ex was married, and she had even heard he was expecting a child soon. It was as if she had totally missed the boat. At this point, she felt she might not ever get married because all the good ones were taken. The ones like AJ. Those were always the first to go. She always thought she was a catch, but date after date, she still had a naked ring finger.

She felt frustrated and angry. She couldn't understand how someone not even as attractive or as successful as AJ's wife had such a decent man.

She cried all the way home and decided to make it an early night.

She knew her mother probably wanted to talk about the service that evening, but she didn't want to be reminded of a day that made her realize how single she was once again.

AJ.

If only she could stop thinking about him. There were so many other things that she had to think about besides some unavailable man.

But maybe they could still be church friends?

Chapter Three
God Is My Man

It was about ten p.m., and Brishelle was still up, working on ideas for the best layout on her website. She wanted to make it more inviting and modern. She thought of hiring a graphic designer and doing away with the layout she had purchased two years ago. She noticed that her readership had gone down slightly. She knew it was because the articles she'd posted had been stale. How many different ways could you talk about Rihanna's red matte lipstick?

However, whenever she posted something about natural hair or relationships, she got more views for the week. Her last relationship blog post about her bad Matchr dates got over 10,000 views in one day. Having little to no luck in love seemed to attract more readers to her blog, but she hated having to acknowledge the fact that a long-term relationship still hadn't worked out for her.

One of her favorite "goals" blogs to follow was a woman who had two children, a handsome husband, and was a cardiologist at one of the best hospitals in the country. She seemed like she had it all. She even had time to dress up her children in adorable outfits, take them shopping, and make lattes in the morning. This woman was also exceptionally beautiful with naturally curly hair that fell all the way down to her butt. Her husband, who was also a doctor, looked like he could have been a model. They had met each other while studying at Yale.

Her blog made her seethe with jealousy, but she couldn't stop visiting because she wanted her life so badly. How did this woman literally get it all and then do it all every single day? It was unfair.

After closing out of the "perfect" woman's blog, the feelings of hopelessness that flooded her when she found out that AJ was married came back with a vengeance. She almost wanted to cry again but decided that it just might be time to go to bed. She noticed that when she started stalking the blogs of "perfect" wives and husbands, she becomes unproductive and should probably just go to bed.

Brishelle decided to check her phone one last time before she went to bed. Maybe there was an email from her business partner in New York who wrote for another online women's magazine.

Her mother had texted her about five times and called her. Her heart almost dropped, but then she remembered that her mother could be extremely dramatic and tends to call over and over until you picked up to talk about absolutely nothing.

She opened the text.

Breezy! I met this nice young man at the laywomen's banquet over at Glory Harvest. He is very handsome and works for the city. He seems like your type. I gave him your number to call you, and I have his number too. It's 323-555-6565. You should talk to him or something. He seems like a nice young man.

Brishelle rolled her eyes so hard, they could have fallen out of her skull.

Her mother NEVER had good taste when it came to men. Her own father, Henry, had had a drinking problem for the past twenty-five years, and she suspected he had cheated on her mother at least once.

Her mother tended to choose the goofiest looking men as potential suitors for her. One time, her mother suggested that she talk to an older man who worked at her job who was looking for a wife. The man was fifty and looked like he could have been her father's age when her mother sent his picture. When Brishelle refused to call him, her mother said she was ungrateful and needed to give the man a chance because he was "saved".

Brishelle decided to give her mother one more chance with her love life because, at this point, she was kind of desperate and her eggs weren't getting any younger. She didn't want to have children after forty or wait until thirty-five. She didn't want to rush anything either, but it was not like she was twenty-five and had time on her hands.

She decided to text her mother back.

OK, momma. I'll talk to him.

She almost cringed when she wrote it.

Her mother texted back almost instantly.

Well, praise God! You'll be married in no time Breezy!

Brishelle always hated how her mother overused religious language and exclamation points through text, but at least she was the only one looking out for her love life. Her best friend Tiera had set her up on a date with a man who lied about having three kids with three different women once. She told Tiera that if she ever set her up on a date with a baby daddy again, their friendship would be over.

Brishelle wanted to wait until tomorrow afternoon to shoot the mystery guy a text but decided to go ahead and send one now.

She hoped he was somewhat good looking. He didn't have to be a GQ model, but at least something she could put up with. She also hoped her mother hadn't set her up with some short man. Her own father was only 5'7, and he never treated her mother right, despite her mother settling for someone under six feet.

Brishelle typed a text that said, **Hey, my mother said she met you at a church function.**

She decided to turn her phone on vibrate and reply in the morning. However, the person on the other end almost immediately texted her back with a reply.

Yes! Your mother told me that your name is Giselle?

Brishelle, she texted hesitantly.

Oh, yes! How are you?

Good, she replied.

Would you like to get a bite to eat sometime?

Brishelle thought about how someone who had only texted about ten words to her felt it was appropriate to ask her out on a date so quickly. He seemed too eager and nice. She hadn't met him yet, but he came off as kind of corny by saying, "get a bite to eat." He sounded like that trombone player in the marching band in high school who would try and write her love letters. She eventually had to tell him to his face that she wasn't interested and hurt his feelings in front of the entire band.

Uh, yeah…that sounds good.

Brishelle knew the guy was probably a certified dork, but she didn't have that many options. She couldn't clearly remember the last time someone had asked her out on a date that wasn't some weirdo on a dating app.

Great! What would you like? Coffee? Tacos?

Coffee? Tacos? What do those two have to do with each other?

Brishelle would rather go to some inexpensive but busy café that she could easily slip out of.

Yeah, um… we could meet at Cora's Café over there on Marlo Street near the church.

Sounds like a great idea, he replied. *What time?*

Oh, around two is fine.

No problem! See ya at two, sweetie!

Sweetie?

They'd had one conversation over text, and he was already giving her pet names? This guy had to be crazy. She hated when men got too familiar over text so soon. But she decided to bite the bullet and give this man a chance. She wanted a man of God over everything. She might be willing to cross a few minor things off her new husband qualification list if he was decent. She didn't want to settle, but she felt as if settling was far better than being single at forty. Maybe she could use him as a placeholder until AJ got divorced.

She tried to block that demonic thought from her mind, but a part of her was still upset that every time she turned around, another eligible Black man was taken. Was it so wrong to secretly lust over AJ?

Her mind drifted toward those sexy, broad shoulders and brown skin. She remembered when she touched his hands and how strong they felt covering hers.

She imagined him on top of her with his shirt off, removing her bra with one hand. She dreamt of finally sucking those soft, full lips under her satin sheets. She knew he definitely had at least seven inches on him, and thick all the way around like the trunk of a tree. She started to mentally undress him and try to feel what it must feel like to have his whole manhood slip inside her moist body.

She then drifted off to sleep while gently massaging her pocketbook, as her mother used to call it.

The next day, Brishelle almost forgot she was supposed to go on a date with the mystery guy. She didn't even know his name. She had forgotten to ask, but she hated that he knew hers. She was sure her mother, who could not keep her mouth shut most of the time, had told him her nickname, too. She never forgave her mother for showing her prom date all her embarrassing childhood pictures right before she was about to make her grand entrance.

decided to text him to see if they were still on.

He said they were.

Fuck, she thought.

She really didn't want to go see this weirdo, but she kept imagining herself in a wedding dress, walking down the aisle of Glory Harvest and kept hope alive for the time being. If he wasn't her type, she could just pass him along to that white girl she used to talk to in college. She probably liked nerdy black men.

She pulled up to Cora's Café, which was a gentrified coffee house in the middle of L.A. It was an eclectic crowd of Black people, white people, some Asian, and Hispanics. Everyone looked kind of artsy and very educated. She overheard two white men loudly argue about something having to do with Republicans but quickly drowned them out while nervously looking for her date.

She decided to just order a coffee, and if she didn't see him in about ten minutes, she would leave.

Suddenly, someone walked up behind her.

"Brishelle?"

She turned around, and it was worse than she thought.

He was past ugly. He was fugly.

The consistent wetness that she had been experiencing from thinking about AJ dried up like Death Valley.

He had thick glasses, acne scars mainly on his cheeks, a patchy beard, a fuzzy hairline that hadn't been lined up in weeks, and slightly yellow teeth. She was even more repulsed at his outfit. He wore a plaid shirt that was tucked into wrinkly khakis and a belt. He looked ashy, and his nose was far too large for his face.

Was her mother trying to play a joke on her or something?

This was the last time she'd ever let anyone close to her or not pick out a blind date for her. This was worse than her luck on Matchr. At least she had an idea of what she expected when she went on there. Once, a man on the app surprised her because he was at least five inches shorter than he reported, but she went on with the date anyway. She just never called him again.

She was now almost infuriated that this sorry excuse for a man had her number. However, a piece of her felt bad for him, so she decided to try and make it through the date. He seemed nice, so maybe he could be a nice friend.

She found out that he was actually a corporate lawyer. He was only twenty-eight and already owned his home. He had no children, but he had a French Bulldog named "Rocko". He loved to travel and had been to eight countries already, including Japan and Egypt. He enjoyed skiing and went to the gym regularly. He had never been married before.

Well, if he didn't look like wet trash, he'd be a catch. He had everything she wanted on paper, so she could now see why her mother would push someone like this on her. However, she just couldn't see herself settling.

He also talked about himself too much, which kind of turned her off, but then, she was starting to think that she was just finding any excuse she could to not continue dating him.

She tried her best to act interested but then became bored of listening to him talk about all his accolades. It seemed like everything she said about herself, he always had something to match, but better.

"I went to UCLA," she said.

"Oh, really? I went to Brown and then Harvard Law," he replied.

"I exercise about twice a week," she said meekly.

"I exercise an hour a day!"

She began to get very tired of listening to how perfect he was. I guess it was to make up for being so ugly, and probably having a small dick.

After they talked for about two hours, Brishelle pretended to have gotten an emergency text from work. She told him she had to leave immediately. Her graphic designer seemed to have messed up something important on her page, and she needed to meet with him ASAP.

"I-I'm so sorry we have to cut it short. I'll keep in touch, though. It was nice meeting you," Brishelle stammered.

"That's OK, hun! We should meet up later this week."

"Yeah, sure," Brishelle lied.

He attempted to give her a hug. She gave him one of those church hugs where you don't quite touch each other, but it's just enough affection to know that you still tolerate the other person.

She walked out of the café quickly. It wasn't the absolute worst date of her life, but it was pretty close. She felt like she had wasted two hours of her time just by trying to be nice. She wanted to leave thirty minutes in, but she thought about him going back and telling her mother about it, so she refrained. The last thing she wanted was a lecture about how she didn't even stay on dates long enough to get to know the man.

She had even forgotten his name. She didn't really try to remember it. It must have been Ricky or something. He was so busy talking about himself, it was information overload.

She decided to not text her mother about how the date had gone because she was in the mood to be brutally honest.

This was frustrating.

Before driving home, she decided to pick up something to eat at a local Thai take-out place. It seemed like there were certainly Black men who were alive and available all around. They were just too busy trying to sell mixtapes, lay out bootleg copies of DVDs on the ground, and harass anyone who dared walk in front of the liquor store they were congregating in front of. Brishelle tried to avoid ghetto mini-markets and strip malls whenever she could, but the Thai place was located in one, and it was her favorite spot. Like clockwork, a few dirty looking hustlers were in front of the Thai place, either begging for change or to buy their mixtape.

Brishelle always told herself that she would look forward without paying attention to anyone, get her food, and leave.

This rarely worked out as well as she expected.

"Damn, baby!"

"Hey, Brown Skin!"

All of a sudden, the catcalls came at her like a ton of bricks falling off a dilapidated chimney.

Brishelle hurried into the Thai restaurant to order her favorite dish, Chicken Pad Thai. She could sense the men outside ogling her with their droopy, smoked-out eyes. It disgusted her that she got so much attention from the wrong men and not enough attention from the right men. She couldn't remember the last time a man with straight, white teeth and a nine-to-five went out of their way to get her number in public.

Maybe Tiera was right. Maybe L.A. was the worst place to find a man. But AJ was here, and there just absolutely had to be someone else like him out there. He couldn't possibly be the only one.

On her way home, Brishelle could feel the tears starting to well up in her eyes again. She thought she was probably just going on her period and that she was taking everything too seriously.

When she finally arrived home, she decided to call up Tiera to vent. She must have cried on the phone for two hours until Tiera calmed her down.

"Girl, it's just not fair!"

Brishelle was inconsolable.

"What's not fair? That you can't find a man?"

Tiera didn't seem to be of much help, but Brishelle didn't have anyone else who was just as close to her to vent to. Her mother would just tell her to get over it and that there were plenty of men out there.

"Yes! Basically, it's because my ass is still single. I went on a horrible date with this dude my mom set me up with. It's like the only qualifications she's looking for are 'saved and sanctified'."

"Girl, those are the worst ones," Tiera chimed in.

"I know," Brishelle said meekly.

"So, who was this dude? What he look like?"

"Girl…ugly and weird."

Tiera's laugh sounded like a wild Hyena.

"Girl, I almost dropped my phone. How weird? Because we know how you are. You hate everybody. You thought the dude I set you up with was fugly, too, and he was decent."

"Just trust me when I tell you this one was tragic," Brishelle joked.

While on the phone, she got a text from her mother asking how the date went. She told her how horrible it was, and he wasn't nearly as handsome as she had expected.

Her mother scolded her for being picky and difficult. She told her daughter that she'd never find a husband if she wouldn't stop comparing everyday men to models.

Brishelle decided to not respond to her mother and put the text thread on mute so it would stop alerting her. At this point, she didn't know if she wanted a man at all anymore because the process was much too stressful.

Brishelle put the phone back up to her ear after quickly closing the texting app on the screen.

"Yeah, girl, I'll just wait until that fine-ass keyboardist and his wife break up," Brishelle joked.

"Girl, you crazy!"

"No, I'm just playing. But right now, God is my man," Brishelle answered quickly.

"Girl, you sound like them old church ladies!" Tiera shrieked.

"I'm serious, girl! I'm getting saved and sanctified. I'm dedicating my life to God… I know you rolling your eyes at me."

Brishelle was somewhat serious about her statement, but figured she had to dedicate her life to something besides work and looking for a man.

Brishelle mentally vowed to read her bible every day, go to church every Sunday, pray at least twice daily, and pay her tithes.

When she returned home, she sat on her bed with the lights off and pictured AJ's strong but gentle body shielding her from the world. She began to touch herself gently and vigorously until she came. If she couldn't have AJ, then maybe she would in her dreams.

Chapter Four
Sang Brishelle!

Overloaded with deadlines and new creative projects, Brishelle wasn't as in tune with her love life as she had been before. She decided she'd rather drown herself in her work than to think about how single she felt. She also decided that rededicating her life to God was the best thing she could do for herself right now. She decided she was going to attend church every Sunday, and had even prayed this morning when she got out of bed.

She was starting a new chapter in her life, with or without a man. She felt being single was just a season, and God would bless her eventually, as long as she lived right by Him.

She deleted all the dating apps off her phone and stopped answering the private messages on social media from potentials. It hadn't worked out for her in the past, so it was time to give it up. She had been getting so frustrated on those apps that at one point, she began to swipe right on men she wasn't even that attracted to. One time, she swiped right on a Middle Eastern man who looked somewhat decent. She wasn't into interracial dating at all, so she knew that once she went down that path, it was time to log off.

She had even decided to go and audition for the choir. Although she was swamped with work, she needed a release, and music had always done that for her. She loved those old songs that her mother and grandmother used to sing. She was still nervous about possibly doing a solo, but she knew that as a new choir member, they wouldn't push her up to do a solo so soon.

On Thursday night, at seven-thirty p.m., Brishelle began to get ready for choir rehearsal. She wore a simple black dress that fell down to her knees and a red sweater. She had black ballet flats in her closet that she only wore to interviews, but she felt they would be appropriate for a church event.

When she entered the parking lot, she could hear some of the choir members warming up their voices. They already sounded amazing, and they weren't even singing an actual song. They began singing a congregational song when Brishelle walked in the sanctuary.

I get joy when I think about…
What He's done for me!
Oh I get joy when I think about…
What He's done for me!
Oh you can't tell it let me tell it…

She wished she had walked in from the side door instead of the front door because now she had to walk all the way down the aisle and get stared at by some of the choir members' kids, and then some of the choir members themselves.

The choir consisted of both men and women, including a very feminine choir director. Most of the women were overweight, and the men were either old or clearly played for the other team.
One of the women, who was almost obese, kept staring at Brishelle as if she had stolen something from her. She had a smirk on her face and quickly rolled her eyes at Brishelle. Brishelle almost rolled her eyes back, but then AJ got up from behind the organ to introduce her to the choir.

She could barely see AJ when she walked in. She hadn't even noticed he was there because she was so busy concentrating on who was and who wasn't staring at her.

"All right, choir, we have a new member. Treat her right, y'all! Her momma been a member here for years."

If Brishelle weren't brown-skinned, you would have been able to see her blush.

She loved how he had taken up for her in order to make her feel more comfortable coming to choir rehearsal. However, she didn't know if she was ready to become an actual member yet.

AJ then continued.

"Brishelle, why don't you lead a li'l congregational song, so we know what you sound like."

Brishelle's heart was really racing now. She wasn't prepared to sing alone in front of a bunch of strangers. She thought she would audition individually, or just blend in with the rest of the choir.

"Are you a soprano or alto?" he questioned.

"I'm a soprano, but I do alto parts sometimes," Brishelle said shyly.

"Then let's hear that pretty soprano. We can never have enough sopranos in the choir," AJ joked.

Almost instantly, the soprano section in the front row turned around to stare at her. They didn't seem to be smiling or frowning. However, there was one soprano who refused to turn around. It was AJ's wife, who she recognized from the first time she had come back to Glory Harvest. She could already feel the jealousy, but she knew she had done nothing wrong. Maybe she could sense she had been having dirty thoughts about her husband.

Brishelle decided to close her eyes and sing and pretend that it was just her and AJ.

Jesus I'll never forget what you've done for me
Jesus I'll never forget how you set me free
Jesus I'll never forget how you brought me out

Jesus I'll never forget…oh never!

When she opened her eyes, both AJ and the choir director's eyes lit up. She could tell she was doing good, and of course, the whole choir joined in, including AJ's wife. She was relieved that she only had to sing on her own for about a minute, but she was confident that she had won the choir over.

Brishelle had always been told that she had a voice like a nightingale. She could sing circles around other kids her age when she was a teenager. She was always given lead parts in the school choir growing up. She never experienced much jealousy or competition back then since most of the kids didn't want to be given a solo part anyway. However, she knew that at church, giving away lead parts to songs was stiff competition. There was always that one soprano who thought they were the best singer in the choir. They sang the loudest and always told everyone else how to sing their parts. The church would usually back them up and overpraise them as if they were the second coming of Jesus, and it seemed like AJ's wife, Tasha, was *that* soprano.

AJ's wife wore tight jeans and a V-neck shirt that fit her body very snugly. She had on loud, pink lipstick that clashed with her complexion. Brishelle could see that she had green eyes that appeared to turn hazel, depending on what light she was in. She might have been pretty when she was a lot thinner, but seemed to have let herself go. She wasn't built like some of the pretty, larger women she'd seen who knew how to carry their weight. His wife seemed kind of sloppy.

"Why don't you join the soprano section?" the choir director said.

"Tasha, she can stand next to you today. I like to put my newbies next to my strong singers to help them get better."

Tasha hesitantly moved over.

Brishelle carefully tried to glide past the other singers in the soprano section so she could stand next to Tasha. It felt awkward, and Brishelle wondered if she should have ever come to choir rehearsal in the first place.

She tried to smile at Tasha, who quickly looked away with a weak grin.

Brishelle knew better than to try to make friends with her because she probably knew that everybody was eyeing her man.

Brishelle tried to think of she and AJ as being business partners in music. She would only talk to him about music and music only. She would refrain from flirting or showing any kind of interest.

She took one last look at him as he turned around to sit on the organ and play a song. He even had a little booty on him to hold up his pants. It wasn't too big, but he definitely looked like he worked out. She even noticed how his arms bulged out of the sleeves of his shirt. She loved men with nice arms. He looked like he could pick her up and throw her over his shoulder. She wished he would turn around again, so she could see the dick print. A nice, meaty dick print in a pair of slacks always told her everything she needed to know about a man.

AJ got on the organ and began to play a song she didn't know the words to. The choir director passed her a piece of paper with the lyrics. She read it quickly, but the music had already started playing, and everyone seemed to know what to do.

Brishelle tried to follow, but eventually, just stopped singing. The choir director didn't seem to notice her. He was too busy almost doing some kind of acrobatic moves trying to direct the choir. He spread his arms wide like an eagle with his fists closed to get the music to stop. He stomped his feet and clapped while singing the tenor parts. He was incredibly energetic and seemed to move with the choir like a dancer. He was too much for Brishelle, who grew tired just by looking at him. He was obviously gay, but one of those "don't ask, don't tell" brothers who kept his lifestyle out of the church, but pranced around like a diva. He would be the lone male tambourine player in the pew furthest toward the back, daring any and all women to outplay him.

She moved her attention back to AJ, who caught her eye and she caught his. She smiled. It was a reaction, and she didn't really mean it like that, but it happened. He smiled back and nodded at her. She then quickly turned around before anyone noticed what she was doing.

"Will you be ready to sing a solo this Sunday, Brishelle?" AJ joked over the microphone, while still on the organ.

"No, I don't think so. Not this Sunday," Brishelle tried to say through laughter.

Tasha then looked up at Brishelle and rolled her eyes. Brishelle guessed she thought she had gotten too familiar with her husband too fast, but it was AJ who had asked the question.

"Well, then, hopefully in the next two weeks you will. You have a beautiful voice. My wife needs a little help. She gonna lose that pretty voice of hers one day if she sings every single Sunday."

His wife didn't seem amused, but she cracked a sly smile at her husband.

After they rehearsed the three songs they were going to sing for the service, the choir held hands to pray.

Tasha decided to lead the prayer.

"Lord, we come to You today to ask You to cover us with Your blood. Lord, bless our voices on tomorrow that they may sing Your praises. We want to sing to Your glory and Your honor, Lord. Let no sudden judgment come upon us. You are worthy to be praised! Hallelujah! We give You the glory!"

During Tasha's long-winded prayer, Brishelle opened her eyes to get one last peek at AJ. His eyes were open, too, giving her the most lustful look. She hadn't seen anyone look at her like that since her ex. She was almost startled when she locked eyes with him that she immediately looked away. However, she just couldn't keep her attention off him. He seemed to be undressing her with his eyes. She began to do the same and winked at him. AJ bit his bottom lip and looked back down to close his eyes for the rest of the prayer.

Brishelle couldn't focus on anything else but the exchange that she and AJ had just had. Her pussy started pulsating. If she hadn't worn a very padded bra, she was sure her nipples would be poking straight through her dress.

If she had become that horny from a simple gaze, what could he do to her outside of these four walls? In a car? In her bedroom? She wanted to know so badly, but she had promised to remain celibate and strengthen her relationship with God, and he was also married.

After the prayer, everyone released hands and began gathering their purses and children.

Several children ran around in between the pews, trying to get away from their mothers. It had turned into a zoo as soon as prayer was over.

AJ and the choir director, whose name was Brandon, went into the back together to lock up the church and put the music lyrics away in the choir room.

Brishelle wanted to finally break the ice with Tasha.

"It was nice singing with you today. You have a beautiful voice."

"Mhmm-hmm," Tasha replied.

"I'll see you this Sunday then."

She nodded quickly and turned around to one of the other choir members to ask them if they had seen her tambourine.

Brishelle definitely didn't get warm and fuzzy vibes from her, but she assumed it was due to them not knowing each other well. She knew Tasha might think she was a threat to her, but she didn't necessarily want her husband.

Brishelle thought her husband was fine and had winked at him a little bit, but that was about it. She felt his wife had nothing to worry about. Brishelle then decided to leave it alone and thought the wife was probably just mean to anyone she felt was in competition with her.

On her way out, she spotted AJ coming out of one of the back doors of the church near the dining room. He walked toward her while she was getting in her car.

Brishelle felt her heart racing again. She wanted to know why this man was so interested. He had a wife.

"How was rehearsal?" he said.

"Oh, I enjoyed it. Thank you for inviting me."

The two stared at each other in silence for about three seconds until Brishelle attempted to interrupt the awkwardness.

"You're such a talented organist and keyboardist," Brishelle said coyly.

"Well, you're a talented singer."

His eyes quickly darted from her head to her toes. She immediately felt shivers down her spine. She wanted nothing more than to push him in her car and show him what "talent" looked like.

"Well, I'll see you Sunday," she blurted.

"See you Sunday, love."

Love?

Only her best friend called her "love".

"See you Sunday," she said, crouching to get inside her car.

While inside, she saw him turn around and walk towards his wife, who was just leaving the sanctuary with another woman and a child. She wondered if that child was his.

AJ jogged over to his wife and kissed her on the cheek. The little boy next to the woman appeared to call him Uncle AJ. For some reason, Brishelle was relieved that he didn't have kids. She didn't want to lust after the father of some child who always ran up to hug her after service.

They seemed to be in love, or at least AJ was really good at acting like it. She pulled off from the dark parking lot and headed home.

She wondered if Tiera was busy, but she decided to call her anyway.

"Hello, Tiera?"

"Yeah," she answered on the first ring.

"Yeah, I went to choir rehearsal today," Brishelle said with a sigh.

"Girl! You didn't call me to tell me you went to no choir rehearsal. I know you. Now, who'd you *fuck* at the rehearsal?"

"Girl, wow! Nobody! I just went, and yes, the fine, married dude was there, but I didn't do nothing. I kept my distance."

"Uh-huh…I guess," Tiera said.

"Why you don't believe me?"

"I do believe you, Brishelle, I just don't believe you went to rehearsal *just* to sing. You went to go look at that man and maybe get a little practice in."

"No, I didn't. I went just to sing. He barely looked at me anyway. But yeah, let me talk to you later 'cause you trippin'," she said angrily.

"Stop getting all in your feelings! But whatever, I'll talk to you later."

Brishelle didn't feel like being accused of doing something she wasn't doing. Besides, AJ had looked at her with bedroom eyes first. She just didn't want to be rude.

Brishelle decided to make it an early night again. She didn't feel like looking at the computer after being exhausted from singing all night. She didn't feel like working, but she did feel like doing a little "research" before she went to bed.

She didn't know what AJ stood for, but maybe he was tagged on the church's social media page. She decided to look up Glory Harvest's page, and it had many of the members and church officials' pictures there. She saw there was an album on the page that was labeled "The Harvest Choir".

Brishelle began searching through the pictures, and she recognized many of the choir members she had seen at rehearsal. The choir director and musicians were included as well. After searching all the way down the album to find a picture that was posted about six months ago, she found AJ. He was gorgeous in pictures, too, and was seen smiling at the camera in the middle of playing something on the piano. She placed her mouse over his face, and all of a sudden, his name popped up.

Alfred Sterling Jr.

She didn't like the name Alfred at all. She didn't think it fit him and liked AJ better. She clicked on his page, and most of it was private, but she could see pictures of his wife and a picture of her holding a baby. She clicked on it, and the caption read, "My nephew." She was somewhat relieved but felt a burst of jealousy all over again as she clicked on all their pictures as a couple. He didn't look like he was very in love. She always seemed to be hugging him and smiling a lot harder than he was. However, he didn't appear to be upset, either. He seemed like he tolerated her. She thought maybe she was reading into the pictures too much or applying her own theories, but she used to do this with her friends, and she was almost always right.

She was elated that she could now stalk his social media whenever she wanted to. However, she wished she could see more pictures of him alone, but she would have to send him a request to be his friend for that to happen. She never wanted him to know she had found his profile. If he added her, then maybe she would add him back, but she would never be the first one to make that move. She also thought about how jealous his wife acted and knew she would have a fit. She decided to keep her distance, but would take a look every now and then when she needed some "bedroom inspiration".

In the morning, Brishelle decided to cut her breakfast short and get right to work. She put out an ad for freelance writers who were interested in contributing to the dating/romance section of her website. She had absolutely nothing else to contribute to that section, but she needed the views on her page to make having all those ads and sponsors worthwhile.

It was a fairly sunny day in Los Angeles. There was a little cloud cover, but in the middle of June, this was pretty good because she had gotten tired of the June gloom. After a couple hours of working, she wanted to walk down to the park by her apartment and get some fresh air.

While in middle of typing out an ad, Brishelle got a text from an unknown number that read: *Hey, this is AJ from church. I got your number from your mother. Would you feel like joining the praise team this Sunday? One of the usual members is going to be out this Sunday, and we need a strong voice.*

Brishelle was both startled and delighted. This was the perfect way to start her day. She finally had this cutie's number.

She wasn't sure if she should text back quickly because then it would seem like she had no life and was really feeling him. She also didn't want to text back too late, or maybe he would lose interest and say never mind.

She decided to wait about five minutes and then text her reply.

I would love to. What time should I be there?

She hesitated to send it, making sure everything was spelled correctly. She didn't want him thinking she was pretty AND ignorant.

She sent the text.

He responded within two minutes. He was already doing better than her ex. Her ex used to take all day to respond, and it used to annoy the hell out of her.

Well, praise God! See you on Sunday, babe!

Babe? Who was he calling "babe"?

She was a little shocked but intrigued at the same time. They had given each other sexy looks during prayer, so she knew he must find her attractive, she just wanted to know why he was moving too fast. Did he usually call women in the choir "babe"? She was sure he didn't, but she didn't want to assume he liked her just as much as she liked him.

On Sunday, Brishelle decided to wear a new outfit she had bought at the mall earlier in the week. It was a shorter dress that fit around her body much tighter than usual. It was red and had a large bow attached to the shoulder. She wore a large, gold-colored necklace that her mother had given her. Her hair was down and straight but parted in the middle. She wore her favorite scent that she usually saved for date nights. She had on red heels that matched her dress perfectly. She had gold earrings and made sure her makeup was on point. She had recently gotten her eyelashes done and had bought a sexy, matte red lipstick to match.

She almost looked like Gabrielle Union.

She grabbed her red clutch and walked out the door. She had some driving flats she decided to throw on to keep her feet comfortable for the time being because her feet already hurt.

She could barely find a parking space when she pulled up to the church's parking lot. She forgot it was the first Sunday of the month, and she had on all red. On First Sunday, you were supposed to wear white, and then take communion towards the end of service. She almost wanted to go back home and change, but she didn't want to be too late to join the praise team.

As soon as she stepped out of the car, a few church ladies tried to hide their looks of disgust, but Brishelle chose to ignore them and keep walking towards the sanctuary. Once she was inside, she saw that Sunday school was still going on, so she sat in the back. It seemed as if the pastor was about to wrap up and close in prayer.

AJ then appeared from the side door and sat in the choir stand behind the pastor and the congregation. He pointed at her and motioned for her to come to the side door. She then walked back out and entered the church from the dining area that was attached. She remembered the dining area led to the choir rooms, the pastor's office, and the children's classrooms for Sunday school.

She walked down the rather dark hallway and began to hear people singing inside a room. She also heard children squealing in one of the classrooms. She was always bored in Sunday school as a child and knew those kids might be restless by now if they had been sitting there for an hour or more.

Before she could knock on the door of the choir room where she heard the singing coming from, AJ walked up from the opposite end of the hallway with a grin on his face.

"I knew I heard some click-clacking of somebody's high heels on the floor," AJ joked.

Brishelle tried to look away and smile.

"Yeah, the other members are practicing for the praise team in there. You should go join 'em."

AJ bit his bottom lip almost flirtatiously while taking a good, hard look at Brishelle. As she turned around to enter the choir room, he gently put his hand on her butt to almost give her light push in the door. It was the sexiest thing she had felt in a long time. She hadn't expected it, but she sure did like it. This was the first time they had touched since shaking hands.

He knew what he was doing, and now she needed no more clues to tell her that AJ definitely wanted her. He was a flirt, but she hadn't witnessed him do this to any of the other girls. They weren't that cute anyway. He most likely wanted a slim, brown-skinned girl like her. She was sure she was his type.

When she entered the choir room, a few of the women were sitting on the couch with robes on and were too busy staring down at their phones to notice her. The choir director noticed her right away and told her that the praise team was going to sing some old congregational songs. He said she shouldn't be too worried about memorizing them since they were the same old songs sung everywhere.

"Well, maybe I can practice one," Brishelle said nervously.

She still wasn't ready to make her singing debut in front of the entire church. She hadn't yet told her mother she was supposed to be participating on the praise team. She knew her mother would be impressed, but of course, now all their conversations would be related to church, and she wasn't ready for that yet. She had just started getting serious about God a little while ago, and now she was already an official member of the "Harvest Choir".

"Well, let's go over a few!" the choir director said with both his mouth and hands.

He definitely had the "Broke Wrist" syndrome that her mother always joked about growing up. That meant he was a feminine gay man and didn't hide it. A "Broke Wrist" gay man almost literally meant that the man used a bent wrist gesture while speaking or standing. Not all feminine gay men did this, but the choir director, Brandon, sure did. He was more out and proud than most gay men in the church. People most likely ignored his femininity and probably assumed it was due to him hanging around his mother too much when he was a child.

He began to sing.

"Look where He brought me from!
Oh look where He brought me from!
He brought me out of darkness into the marvelous light!
Look where He brought me from!"

He had an amazing voice. He sounded so effortlessly melodic. She harmonized with him and took the lower part. Brandon was almost a higher soprano than she was due to his falsetto.

AJ took a tambourine from off the table and started playing it. He started playing like an old church lady with his nose scrunched up, sticking his butt out. Brishelle started to laugh, and she almost couldn't sing anymore.

"AJ, stop! You play too much!" Brandon yelled.

He had a wide grin on his face when he said it, so AJ would know he didn't mean it.

One of the choir members, a woman who looked to be about seventy and appeared to be the oldest choir member, walked up from behind Brishelle and tapped her on the shoulder.

"What size you wear? We wearing robes today."

"I'm not sure," Brishelle said almost in a whisper.

"Well, baby, you GOT to know your size!"

The woman seemed pushy, but Brishelle knew better than to argue with church people. They could be some of the evilest people around.

"I think I wear a large," she answered.

"Now, baby, you don't wear no large!" The woman pointed at her stomach. "Now, *I* wear a large. You wear a medium cause you not that big."

"Yes, ma'am," Brishelle replied.

"My name is Mother Henderson. I been in this here choir for over fifty years. You sho' do got a pretty voice, too."

She turned around towards the choir robe rack and swiftly pulled out a medium sized choir robe. Brishelle put it on. She was thankful that the choir wore robes today because she would have hated to be the only one not wearing white in the choir stand.

Brandon then introduced Brishelle to the two other praise team members who she would be singing with.

Their names were Tyanna and Kimiesha. They were cousins, and two of the most ghetto girls Brishelle had ever seen in church. They looked to be about twenty-five, and one of them was probably pregnant. They had long, multicolored nails, their red braids fell all the way down to their kneecaps, they had several facial piercings, and both of them seemed to be popping gum at the same time.

"So, ladies, this is your partner for this week. Treat her right, y'all."

"Yeah, uh-huh, we will. You know what we gon' sang?" Kimiesha said.

"I think so," Brishelle said softly.

"Well, OK. So, um, we gon' lead it and you gon' follow, then you gon' lead it. We like to go like one, two, three." Kimiesha pointed at herself, Tyanna, and then Brishelle.

"Yeah, that sounds good. I'm excited!"

"Yeah, uh-huh," the two girls almost said in unison.

"Go on and walk in, ladies!" Brandon yelled from the couch nearest to the door. "It's showtime! Praise the Lord!"

"Praise the Lord!"

Those who were in the choir room almost said it in unison.

Brishelle walked out with Tyanna and Kimiesha. The ladies walked ahead of her, talking and gossiping.

"Girl, but wait! Did you hear about what happened to my homegirl?" Tyanna said.

"Girl, what happened?" Kimiesha replied.

Before any of them could get a word in, the drummer ran past them in a hurry to start the service. He had both sticks in his hands and the snare drum.

Brishelle could hear the organ warming up. She wondered if that was AJ or if he was on the keyboard. She couldn't wait to catch a glimpse of him. He looked so good today. He had on a nice tie with black slacks that fit that booty nicely, as always. His shirt was clean and white, and his dark-brown skin against it made it look even brighter. She remembered how much he towered over her when they met in the hallway even though she was in heels.

The ladies walked up the stairs toward the side door and opened it. They then scurried over to the mic stand like two mice. Brishelle tried to rush behind them. The organ started playing, and when she turned around, it was AJ. She caught his eye, smiled, and quickly turned away.

Her mother was already standing up, and they hadn't even started singing yet.

Suddenly, AJ's wife Tasha joined them and stood next to Brishelle. She didn't look at her. Kimiesha and Tyanna smiled at her and waved. Tasha walked behind Brishelle and quickly gave the cousins a kiss on the cheek. She ignored Brishelle.

Brishelle saw Tasha make eye contact with AJ, and he instantly knew what song to start on.

Her voice almost boomed through the mic, and the crowd joined her.

Jesus said it!
(Jesus said it!)
That believe in me!
(That believe in me!)
The scripture had said it!
(The scripture had said it!)

That outta your belly!
(Outta your belly!)
Outta your belly!
Shall flow!
(Flow!)
Flow!
(Flow!)
Rivers!
(Of living water!)

After Tasha sang the lead a few times, Kimiesha took the lead of the song and then Tyanna.

Tasha then changed the song a few times. Brishelle had no room to take the lead and was a little frustrated but kept on doing backup.

From the organ, AJ abruptly changed the song to something she didn't recognize at first, then she began to recognize the notes. He began to sing in his smooth tenor.

This train is bound for glory this train.
This train is bound for glory this train.
This train is bound for glory,
Don't carry nothin' but the righteous and holy.

This train is bound for glory, this train.

Tasha opened her mouth, but Brishelle decided to take the lead. She sang the song as if she meant it from the bottom of her soul. She sounded like her mother used to when she was younger. Her voice echoed throughout the pews, and people started standing up everywhere.
She could tell the people were surprised by how well she sounded. She was not only pretty, but she could sing, too.

Tasha quickly took the lead after Brishelle paused for a second. She began to try and out-sing her. She used runs and high notes that Brishelle hadn't incorporated into her singing yet. She didn't feel like she had to "show out" when she knew she could sing.

As soon as Tasha began to sing, Brishelle noticed the organ getting louder and louder. It almost drowned out Tasha and everyone else who sung in the church.

Tasha, Kimiesha, and Tyanna seemed to have figured that the music was too loud, so they temporarily stopped singing and started clapping their hands.

Brishelle decided to take the mic again and began another song.

> *What a mighty God we serve!*
> *What a mighty God we serve!*
> *Angels bow before Him!*
> *Heaven and earth adore Him!*
> *What a mighty God we serve!*

AJ began to incrementally lower the sound of the organ until it was soft enough to hear Brishelle's brilliant soprano. After she sang, Tasha took the lead and sang the song in her version. Not to be outdone, she used some runs that could have sent Luther Vandross packing.

AJ upped the volume on the organ and looked away when Tasha looked back at him. She knew what he was doing, and Brishelle did, too. She was delighted that AJ was taking her side since his wife had been rude to her for no reason. She really had no reason to dislike her. Everything Brishelle had done wrong to Tasha had been limited to her imagination since Brishelle only had unholy thoughts about her husband, but she had never acted upon them.

The four women then gave their testimony as soon as the music died down. Tasha decided to go first, then Kimiesha and Tyanna said their testimonies. All of them were grateful for a new day and being able to praise Him. It was the same old testimony Brishelle had heard a million times.

Brishelle then decided to say her testimony.

"First giving honor to God, who is the head of my life, the pastor, his wife, and to all the saints. I just want to thank God for saving me and giving me life and strength. My God is so awesome and gives me the opportunity to praise His name. I didn't have to make it to Sunday, but here I am, and I thank Him. All the power and glory belongs to Him, and I shall always give Him the praise!"

The membership whooped and hollered while she delivered her testimony. She even heard someone say, "Preach, sista!" and "Gon' talk for the Lord!"

Brishelle wasn't looking directly at them, but she could sense that the other ladies in the praise team were jealous. She had always been able to captivate people when she spoke so she couldn't help it. If they hadn't been so busy bragging about what they had received this week, then they probably would have gotten more people to get with them, too. She thought that some people used testimony service to brag about how much money they had or how saved they were.

After the praise service was done, Brishelle went back up to the choir stand. Kimiesha, Tyanna, and Tasha went in the opposite direction on the other side of the choir stand. Brishelle felt her throat getting a little dry and went through the side door on the left side of the choir stand to go to the water fountain.

She didn't notice AJ had gotten up from the organ as soon as they had stopped singing. She passed by the choir room to get over to the water fountain that was near the dining area. She saw that the choir room's door was open, and when she peeked inside, AJ was sitting on the couch towards the back of the room, texting.

"What you doing texting instead of playing the organ?" Brishelle joked.

His deep, ebony eyes looked up at her, and he had the biggest smile on his face. All the lust she had felt for him came rushing back. His legs were spread wide open while seated, and his phone was in between his muscular hands, resting on each thigh. He had taken his tie off and had one button open to reveal a little bit of his chest. It was only a tiny peak of it, but it still looked sexy to her.

"Just checking some emails, love. What you doing back here?"

She felt his eyes start at her face, then trail down to her breasts. She was already focused on that package of his that leaned to the side in his black slacks.

There was so much sexual tension in the room already, and she had just been in there a few seconds.

"Well, I'm just gonna go get some water," Brishelle said, trying to turn away.

AJ got off the couch and walked towards her. He put his hands gently around her waist. His big hands almost went around all twenty-six inches.

"Why don't you stay in here for a little bit. The choir doesn't sing for another half-hour." He pulled her body closer to his. He then kissed her gently on the forehead.

"Oh, I don't think we should be doing this," she whispered.

"I'm just being a good friend and trying to keep you comfortable," he said with a sly smile.

"You know you have a wi—" He put his finger to her lips before she could say any more.

"Shhhhh." He took his finger from her mouth to lock the choir room door.

He then pushed her against the wall and kissed her passionately. He bit her tongue, licked her neck, and she bit his bottom lip. She had her arms around his neck and slightly spread her legs a little wider, so she could feel his hard dick near her lady parts. AJ then began to smoothly unbuckle his belt and unzip his pants. She looked down and could see the band of his Polo Ralph Lauren underwear. She lifted her skirt and allowed him to grind on her with his penis still in his underwear, and her very wet panties still on.

"Maybe we shouldn't be doing this," she softly gasped.

He ignored her and began to take the rest of it out his boxer briefs. It was one of the biggest dicks she had ever seen. He had to be at least eight inches, and he was thick all the way around. She didn't think she was ready to take all that.

He then lifted her up with her legs still straddling him and carried her toward the couch. He put two fingers on her panties and began rubbing it vigorously until she got even wetter. He then pulled his boxers down and exposed his manhood. He rubbed the tip on her to get ready to enter.

"Ay, AJ! They need you!"

Someone knocked on the door with two heavy bangs of their fist.

"Oh, all right, bro. I was just taking a nap!"

AJ put his dick back in his pants and zipped up his slacks.

Brishelle was afraid of being caught by whoever was at the door. She quickly pulled her panties up and pulled her dress down. She told him not to open the door yet.

"He's gone, love, don't worry. I would never put you in a position like that. Except for the one I just put you in." He stuck out his tongue playfully.

She narrowed her eyes and gave him a smirk.

"Well, I'm still thirsty."

"I bet you are," he joked. "I'll see you in there. Study those songs."

He put his tie back on, kissed her on the forehead and slowly jogged in the direction of the sanctuary.

She decided to lay on the couch a little bit longer and take in all that had just happened to her. Whoever that was had interrupted the beginning of possibly the best sex of her life. She then felt somewhat bad about doing it in the church, but she figured it was the choir room, and not the sanctuary, so it wasn't as bad.

Brishelle returned to the sanctuary about fifteen minutes later. She had left her robe in the choir stand because she felt like she had overheated from singing on the praise team.

The choir sang two more songs before the pastor was to give his afternoon sermon.

Brishelle tried to avoid direct eye contact with AJ the entire time. She started to feel a little guilty about what they had done in the choir room.

His wife was beginning to warm up to her a little. She offered Brishelle a peppermint and gave her the lyrics to the songs they were going to sing prior to singing them.

After the sermon, the pastor ended the service with an altar call. This was the portion of the service where those who were not saved were asked to come and receive Jesus as their Lord and Savior and then ask for forgiveness for their sins. Typically, this was the part of the service for the alcoholics, drug abusers, and single mothers to come up to the altar. Everyone who at least "acted" saved in church wouldn't dare expose themselves for fear of being outed as a sinner.

Brishelle felt differently this Sunday. The guilt of having almost slept with a married man began to creep up on her. No one knew, of course, but she wanted to be released from this shame and ask for forgiveness since she had basically sinned in the Lord's house. If someone had done something wrong at her apartment, she'd want them to apologize, too.

Brishelle noticed that there were more people than usual at the altar, including her own mother, which made her feel much better about joining.

The pastor dipped his finger in olive oil to create a cross on her forehead and prayed for her.

"Do you confess that Jesus is your Lord and Savior!" the pastor shrieked.

"Yes, I do!" she replied.

"Help her, Lord! Honduh-bashunda-boga!" The pastor began speaking in tongues.

Brishelle began speaking in tongues, and before she knew it, the pastor pushed her forehead back, and she fell out on the floor near the altar. An older woman covered her with a large white cloth from the waist down.

When she awoke about five minutes later, she noticed another man on the organ. AJ stood next to her, clapping his hands. He helped her stand up. Brishelle tried not to look at him while she walked back up to the choir stand.

Before she walked up the stairs that led to where the choir was seated, an older woman of about eighty tapped her on the shoulder.

"Now, baby, you know that dress was too short to wear to God's house."

She wanted to tell the woman off right then and there, but she had already committed enough sins in the church for one day, and she had always been told to respect her elders.

Brishelle decided she'd had enough and decided to leave church early. She put her robe back in the choir room and headed out of the back door.

She jetted towards her car and turned on the engine. In her rearview mirror, she noticed AJ walking out the church's back door. He looked like he was trying to wave her down and talk to her, but she backed out quickly and ignored him.

Maybe I'll take off next Sunday, she thought. God would understand.

Chapter Five
The Sopranos

Brishelle decided to skip church for a couple of Sundays. She felt like she needed to refocus herself after what had happened. AJ had texted her recently to ask where she'd been, but she just texted him back and said she was on a business trip and would be back soon. She didn't understand why he was concerned about her because he had a wife to attend to.

After the second missed Sunday, she received a text from her mother.

Now, Brishelle. You was doing good and now you not comin' to church no more.

Momma, I've been busy. I think I'll come next Sunday, Brishelle replied.

You think, or you know?

Brishelle decided not to respond.

Recently, she hadn't been getting as many views and comments on *HeyBlackGrl!*

She wondered if there was just so much more competition these days, or maybe her articles and pictures weren't as intriguing.

She began to write a short article on how to get your boyfriend to propose. She knew nothing about proposals, and barely knew much about boyfriends, but she had studied enough articles on that topic to guide her.

Until she found a romance/lifestyle writer, she would do it herself. She had past experiences with relationships, but she hadn't been in a long-term relationship in about four years.

While out of church, Brishelle had been working on her walk with God by praying more often and reading the bible. She had The Bible app on her phone and used it daily for inspiration or meditation. She was finally beginning to feel good about life, and she felt as if she was finally finding her purpose. She was glad that she had taken a short break from church to get herself together. She promised to stay out of drama when she returned. She wouldn't talk to

AJ, and she would be nice to his wife despite how she treated her. She was going to always treat others the way she wanted to be treated.

She didn't plan on shouting down the aisles anytime soon during service, but she did plan on being more involved. She wanted to get more involved with the youth and the church's charitable foundations. She also promised to always pay her tithes. She used to hate giving money in church when she was younger because she felt like it wasn't going anywhere but to the pastor and the people who worked for him. Fortunately, she felt a lot more charitable these days and was willing to be less selfish and more open as Jesus was.

So, you coming this Sunday? Brishelle got an unexpected text from AJ on Friday night.

Why does it matter to you? she replied.

Well damn lol. I just wanted to know if my best soprano was gonna make it. Don't gotta gimme all that.

Brishelle rolled her eyes. She was supposed to be over him, but a little piece of her still wanted a little male attention from time to time.

I'm coming this Sunday, so don't worry, Brishelle texted back quickly.

Well, good, because we miss you!

Who's 'we'? I think it's you who misses me, she texted.

He then sent a winking emoji.

That winking emoji could have meant anything, but it definitely came off as flirtatious. She liked it, but she wouldn't send anything back. He was a married man, and she had sworn off flirting with him. However, she wanted to know why he was so interested. Did he see something past the way she looked? Did he secretly wish he could be with a more ambitious woman?

She didn't even know what he did for a living besides play the keyboard. He could be a bum for all she knew. He sure would be a fine-ass bum, though.

On Thursday evening, Brishelle was a little tired, but she decided to go to choir rehearsal anyway. She wanted to sing on Sunday, and they might have an issue if she came on Sunday to sing but didn't practice. She knew how Black people could sometimes be. Even though all the songs they were going to sing had been sung over 10,000 times in the last ten years, they'd still roll their necks if they saw her show up to sing during Sunday service, having skipped Thursday night rehearsal.

When she arrived at the church, there were fewer cars than she remembered from last time. She decided to wear jeans and a t-shirt this time. She didn't feel like being on display. She still looked gorgeous. Her hair was in a ponytail with a few strands of hair coming down around her face for the "messy" look, and she had a salmon-colored lipstick on that went beautifully with her complexion. She wore wedge heels with tight jeans to give off that "I actually tried but I don't want to look like I did" look.

When she arrived inside, the choir members were sitting around, talking and laughing. Kimiesha and Tyanna were sitting in the audience, trying to keep track of their unruly children who were jumping on the pews.

"Sit'cho ass down, Day'Kari!" Kimiesha screamed.

Everyone was quiet for a few seconds, staring at Kimiesha in shock.

"I shoulda left you wit yo' granny! You never know how to act!"

"Just leave 'em there, baby. We gotta start rehearsal," Sister Jenkins, the choir member who most resembled a mother figure, said.

Brishelle walked up to the choir stand to sit next to the other members. They still didn't seem to have warmed up to her, but she sat in the soprano section anyway.

She hadn't seen AJ anywhere yet. She wanted to know why he had asked her to come if he hadn't even shown up. She wondered if he was just arriving late.

The choir director walked in from the side door of the church.

"All right, saints! Sorry I'm late, but let's get those voices warmed up."

The choir members stood up almost at once and began singing a traditional congregational song. They were able to instantly harmonize their voices. Brishelle was trying to see where she fit in since she had never practiced the song like this before. They had figured out how to do a three-part harmony for "What A Mighty God We Serve." Brishelle thought Black people would make anything complicated even when it didn't have to be.

Brishelle began singing along and thought she knew what to do.
"Hold on, stop!" One of the choir members raised her tambourine in the air.

"Somebody's off, 'cause this is not how we usually sing these parts."

Brishelle knew it was her, but she didn't want to say anything. She was doing the best she could, but they were making a simple song unnecessarily complicated.

"It might be me, Brandon. I don't know how you guys are doing these parts. I guess I was doing to alto part," Brishelle almost stuttered.

"It's OK, honey. Let's do it without you for a second, and then we gon' teach you a little later."

The choir sang together again, but this time, in perfect harmony, excluding Brishelle.

Brishelle felt embarrassed but then attempted to pretend to look on her social media timeline instead of singing along. She wished she had never come.

After a few minutes of listening to way overdone church songs, AJ and his wife walked in. All of a sudden, everyone said, "Hello," and "Hey, girl." They were greeted like a king and queen. It made Brishelle a little envious. She wished she could walk in some place with her loving

husband trailing behind her. It was so much better than
going everywhere alone.

After the congregational warm-up songs were done,
Tasha wanted to introduce a new choir song. Brishelle was
still very irritated by his wife. She seemed like she thought
she knew everything. She was certainly not the best voice
Brishelle had ever heard. She could sing well, but that
didn't mean it gave her the green light to tell everybody
what to do.

"OK, choir," she started. "We gonna sing 'Great Is
Your Mercy' by Donnie McClurkin. Y'all know that
song?"

"Yes!" the choir quickly responded.

Tasha wore a rather old baseball t-shirt and baggy
jeans. Her long braids were in a sloppy bun towards the
back. She wasn't wearing any makeup, and her face looked
dry. Brishelle thought that a little chapstick could go a long
way. She looked like she had rolled out of bed.

"OK, well I'm gon' lead, and y'all follow. It's real easy."

Tasha began singing in her almost opera-like soprano. She definitely had a beautiful voice, which could be unexpected since she looked like somebody had knocked her out with a wrecking ball before she arrived.

The choir passed around several sheets that had the lyrics printed on them. Brishelle took her copy. She had heard this song several times before, so she didn't think she'd have to look at the paper.

The song required the lead to sing the verses twice, and then a representative of each section, of which included the sopranos, altos, tenors, and bass, to sing the song in their own way.

When Tasha was done singing, she handed the mic to Tyanna, an alto.

AJ, who was on the keyboard, abruptly stopped playing.

"Now, Tasha, give Brishelle the mic first. We're starting with sopranos."

Tasha gave a look that was sharp enough to slice bread.

"Now I know when I married you, the vow said, 'to obey'," AJ said with a Kool-Aid smile.

Brishelle felt like she had been put on the spot, but she was relieved that AJ had stood up for her. However, the fact that he was telling his wife to "obey" kind of rubbed her the wrong way, but she brushed it off. She liked men who confidently stated their opinions. She always hated passive aggressive men like her ex. He wouldn't stand up for what he believed in if she tried to strangle it out of him.

AJ began the song again from the top. Tasha sang her verses alone, then begrudgingly gave the mic over to Brishelle. Brishelle sang the verse like a songbird. The notes seemed to glide around the empty pews into the ears of anyone who was listening.

After she was done, the choir began to clap before they sang the verses in harmony. After the song was done, the other choir members couldn't stop expressing how beautifully Brishelle sang. Tasha was obviously jealous but managed to crack a disingenuous smile.

Tasha was asked to lead the praise team service and the entrance song for the pastor and wife's anniversary service entitled, "Give Me My Flowers." This song was usually sung prior to the pastor and wife's anniversary service so they could walk down the aisle and greet the members. Anniversary services were a big deal as Brishelle remembered. Local churches from all over would come to support the anniversary of the pastor and wife's annual celebration of becoming the Glory Harvest's "shepherds".

Brishelle glanced at AJ from time to time during rehearsal, but he didn't glance back at her as often. He seemed nice at the beginning of the rehearsal, but all of a sudden, he seemed to be more attentive to his wife. He gave his wife an unusual number of compliments as she sang. He wasn't smiling at Brishelle directly anymore, and he almost seemed to avoid eye contact. He gave his wife several kisses while on the keyboard after rehearsal was over, which made some of the other choir members shout, "Aww!"

Brishelle was jealous, but she knew she had no right to be. She wanted to know why he was acting like this when he had been singing a different tune a couple of weeks ago. Was he trying to throw his wife off the scent of their interest in each other?

As the choir packed up their things, Brishelle decided to quickly get her purse and smoothly brush past AJ while he was putting up the keyboard.

He didn't seem to notice her, and instead, decided to grab his wife around her waist and dip her as if they were dancing. He said, "Now y'all look at my pretty li'l thang here! It's almost our anniversary!"

"Stop, babe!" Tasha blurted with a smile.

"No, baby! I want everyone to know I'm with this beautiful woman, and I won't let no man or woman come against us! Praise God, church?"

"Praise God!" shouted the choir members who were left gathering their things.

Brishelle was baffled. Was he trying to call her out in front of everyone? She wondered if they knew anything about what they had done in the choir room. She wondered if he had told his wife. She was fuming.

He had never been this lovey-dovey with his wife, and it seemed rather fishy. Was he trying to throw off his wife or her?

Brishelle quickly rolled her eyes at him, grabbed her purse, and almost swiftly walked out the church without looking at anyone.

She was hurt that he wanted to pretend as if she didn't exist. She did feel bad about what she had done, and she knew she shouldn't be sneaking around with a married man, but she felt she could at least be acknowledged.

She decided to swear him off forever. She would go to church next Sunday, but it would be her last time because she thought he was nothing but a punk. He didn't have to own up to what they had done, but he shouldn't be pretending that it had never happened. She now knew that was probably why his wife couldn't stand her. Her heart was heavy. She wanted to block him on her phone, but she decided against it. He would more than likely get in contact with her mother, and then she'd have to block her own mother.

She drove home in a rage, almost running through two red lights. She had so many tears welling in her eyes, she could barely see.

When she got inside, she threw her purse down and fell out on the couch. She was both extremely upset and exhausted.

She decided she was going to text AJ and give him a piece of her mind. He was not going to throw her under the bus for something they had done together. She was sorry that it had happened, but he needed to acknowledge it and move on.

She opened up her text messages and sent a text to AJ.

Fuck you! You're fake as hell. Don't ever talk to me again. Business only.

She didn't hear from him about twenty minutes, and then he finally replied.

Damn, baby, where'd all this come from? I get home, tryna relax, and read an ugly text from such a pretty lady.

OK, well one, I'm not your baby. Two, how you ignored me today and was acting all lovey-dovey with your wife was uncalled for. You know that wasn't real. Then you said let no woman come against us. You're fucked up, she replied, trying to scroll down her social media, which usually kept her calm when she was upset.

LOL, Brishelle, look...our anniversary is coming up, so you know I gotta be extra. I wasn't even talking about you, so I don't know why you would even say something like that. I know what we did, and I'm not ashamed of it. You're sexy as hell. I was just trying to

make her feel special. I mean, she was dressed like a
homeless person lmfao.

Brishelle couldn't believe he would say that about his wife, but then she assumed that he must think very highly of her. She thought that she was definitely his type, and it was proven through this text.

Well, yeah, I felt some kind of way, Brishelle replied.

LOL, I know you did, but, Brishelle come on. The choir prolly knows that I would wanna be with a fine-ass chick like you instead of my wife. I'm just tryna throw them off. You shouldn't feel any kinda way. I still wanna be cool with each other.

Brishelle felt relieved, but a part of her just wanted him to acknowledge her in public in some way. She knew that would never happen at church, but she craved feeling like a queen in his arms in front of everyone.

Hey, you know next Saturday, not this one, is the church picnic. You should come through. He was texting her back pretty quickly by this point.

Yeah, I'll see. I'm not sure about what I'm doing that Saturday.

I wanna see your fine ass that's why. You know who you was wearing them tight-ass jeans for at rehearsal.

Lol, not for you! she replied.

Bullshit! You been tryna send a nigga to hell since you got there. You ain't shit. I'm tryna get right with God.

Now you know you lying. You wasn't tryin' to get right with God when you locked me in that choir room. Brishelle was texting and getting ready for bed.

So, what you got on? AJ replied.

None of your business, damn. Don't you have a wife?

Damn, why you always gotta go there? Tryna make me feel bad. I know I gotta wife.

You have any kids? She had wanted to ask that for a while.

Naw.

Hmmm, I'm surprised.

Why you surprised?

You just seem like a family man.

Naw, I'm not tryna have kids right now, but we will. I wanna son.

Brishelle had always wanted kids. She wanted at least two and a dog. She loved when men wanted to have a family as well. She never wanted to have kids with a man who already had kids, though.

You got kids?

Uh-uh, I don't. I want some, though.

So, I have one question… Why you so fuckin' fine?

Brishelle rolled her eyes.

Why you so fine? she replied.

Cuz I get it from my momma. That's why.

Boy, stop. You play too much.

You should come see me before Sunday, AJ said with a winking emoji.

I don't know, I can get kind of busy during the week. Besides, I'm not tryna get all caught up with your wife and everything.

, fuck that. I'm tryna see you. I promise I won't do nothing.

He didn't seem very convincing, but this whole text conversation was turning Brishelle on. She wished she could be lying in bed with him right now, whispering this conversation to each other instead of texting it.

Now you know that's not true. We will definitely do something. We already have.

Naw, but we could meet like somewhere more public, AJ replied.

And get caught by your wife or some nosy-ass church members?

I'm not gon' get you caught up, baby.

Brishelle had accepted him calling her baby. She wouldn't give him a pet name anytime soon, but maybe if their relationship progressed, she would.

I'll think about it, AJ. I'm not sure. But I will see you this Sunday to sing.

Hmmm, OK.

I'm 'bout to sleep anyway.

Now you know that's a lie from hell. You not goin' to sleep at 9:30, you just wanna stop texting me. You don't like me like that.

Wow, whatever. Yes, I do. I just have so much to do in the morning, so I need to call it an early night. You probably wouldn't know because all you do is play piano on Sunday.

Oh, you takin shots now? Damn, lol. Naw, but I'm in real estate, and I coach boys' basketball.

Oh OK, so you busy I see.

Hell yeah, lol. I do a lot of shit. I do pretty well for myself.

Brishelle was turned on even more. She loved when a man was confident in his career and financially stable. Her ex was always going from job to job. He could never quite figure out what he wanted to do with his life. AJ was such a great catch. She wondered how she had gotten overlooked in order to not be married to someone like this.

Well, it seems like your wife is a lucky woman.

You lucky, too, bae. He sent a kissing emoji.

Wait, what do you mean?

He didn't respond as quickly as he had been, so she assumed he must have gotten busy right away.

He was so sexy to her even through text. She couldn't resist talking to him. She had sworn to let him go, but he kept pulling her back in with each text and look into her eyes at church. She was supposed to be angry with him, but for some reason, he helped calm her anxieties about their "relationship" and make her very confident, and he definitely had eyes for her. Now she knew more about how he felt about his wife. It almost made her feel bad for her, but she had been so mean, she thought she deserved it.

Brishelle thought his wife must know he had feelings for someone else, she just didn't know it was her.

His wife didn't even try to be attractive, though, so she wondered if she didn't think she had to because he came home every night.

She never pictured herself as someone's mistress, but she was willing to go through with it if it meant he would eventually come to his senses and leave her. It was a wild idea, but she could always have him as a fuck buddy when she was bored.

After she wrapped her hair up to go to bed and put on her night clothes, she faded away to sleep. She was exhausted, but had a calm feeling over her. AJ made her feel special. No man had ever made her feel the way AJ made her feel. She knew it was mostly lust, but she knew that was how most love stories started.

In the middle of the night, while Brishelle was fast asleep, she heard a loud alert from her phone. She tried to open up her eyes to read who it was from.

It was AJ.

Goodnight, babe! he said with a heart emoji at the end.

She wanted to reply, but she decided she would leave him on read for at least a few minutes to look like she had more going for herself than sitting next to her phone. She wanted AJ, but she didn't want him to think she was obsessed with him by answering him within a few seconds of texting her.

She decided it was worth it to stay up for about fifteen minutes. She began scrolling down her social media to pass the time. However, after about three minutes, she became bored and wanted to get it over with.

Goodnight, she said with the same heart emoji at the end.

He immediately sent a kissing face emoji and the tongue emoji.

He was doing the most, she thought, but it was sexy. She didn't want to send him any emoji back that could have expressed how much she wanted him, too, even though she did. She decided to just leave him on read. He kind of deserved it anyway.

She then went back to sleep.

However, thinking about AJ finally fucking the shit out of her turned her on again. She flipped her pillow so it laid vertically underneath her and began rubbing it until she came. She came so hard, she almost screamed. She turned over on the other side of her king-sized bed and tried to calm her breathing. She felt amazing after doing that and couldn't wait until AJ took the place of her pillow. Maybe she would meet up with him someday, but just not within the next two weeks.

Brishelle then put her phone on vibrate and turned over on her side to sleep. She dreamt deeply, her body totally relaxed and naked after having taken her night clothes off before she masturbated.

It wasn't her fault that Tasha's husband was in love with her. She should fix herself up sometimes, and maybe she could hold on to her fine-ass man.

Chapter Six
Sexy but Classy

It was the morning of the pastor and wife's anniversary service. Besides Mother's Day, this was one of the most fashion-forward Sundays of the year. The old church ladies would come dressed to the nines in church hats bigger than their face, and new prayer cloths that they could cover their ankle-length skirts with. Some of the elders in the church might even have on bow ties. She remembered when she was a teenager, some of the men would come dressed to the anniversary service as if they were going to The Oscars. Brishelle knew she had to dress to impress, but not too sexily. She didn't want to make any old ladies upset this time. She wasn't going to wear one of those church suits she had always hated, but she was going to wear a nice, classy dress for the occasion that made her look like a million bucks without trying. She thought it was better to accessorize than to overdress.

Brishelle wore a black A-line dress that almost touched her knees. She had a chunky gold necklace on and gold heels. She wore a gold-colored clutch as well. She made sure she looked in the mirror several times, just to make sure everything was perfect. Her hair was down and bone straight, but parted to the side. She even wore false eyelashes to give herself a bit of extra flair. She knew she would get plenty of attention anyway, no matter what she wore, but this time, she didn't feel the need to show off her Coke bottle shape. She would save that for the picnic next week.

When she arrived at the church, she noticed AJ's car was parked in the same spot it always was. She decided to park next to him just in case it was hard to find him after service. She walked in through the back door of the church and headed toward the choir room. When she got in, the choir director looked flustered.

"Brishelle! I couldn't wait until you got here. We need you to lead the anniversary service songs. This morning, I'll lead the songs and direct, but you just need to sing 'Give Me My Flowers' and 'Great Is Your Mercy' this afternoon."

Brishelle was shocked. She didn't know what to think. She thought Tasha was in charge of leading those songs. She was also the newest choir member and didn't understand why they would choose her out of all the choir members.

"But, Brandon, I thought Tasha was leading those songs," Brishelle said meekly.

"No, she's out with a cold. She's real hoarse. She can't talk."

Part of Brishelle was upset that she'd have to take the lead on a song she didn't know that well, but part of her was also relieved that Tasha wasn't there. At least she could sit in the soprano section in peace.

"So, make sure you practice, hun…but you'll be fine. I'm sure you've heard 'Give Me My Flowers' a million times."

She really hadn't.

She used to purposely skip afternoon services by the time she became a teenager. She thought they were a waste of time and boring. She usually had had enough church by the time one o'clock hit on Sunday afternoon.

AJ walked in looking about as fine as a Black male model. He had on a full suit this time with a silver tie and a matching silver handkerchief in the pocket. The suit was fitted, but it looked amazing on him. He had black shoes on that looked expensive. She thought they looked a lot like a pair of Bruno Maglis, which could be hundreds of dollars if you didn't find them on sale. Her favorite accessory on a man was his watch, and AJ had on big, gold one that hung off his wrist in a very refined way. It looked expensive, too. He had managed to grow out his beard a little, and it neatly tapered his face as if he had gotten it done at the barbershop. His hair was cut in a nice fade. AJ had beautiful, long eyelashes that framed his mysteriously dark eyes. His lips looked smooth to the touch, and he smelled like some of the best cologne you could buy.

Brishelle was stunned. She wondered how somebody this fine would even think to spend their afternoon at a small church. He looked like he should be acting, or at least a keyboardist at one of those mega churches.

AJ's eyes darted to Brishelle and quickly looked her up and down while the rest of the choir shuffled around, getting ready. Brishelle wished she had worn a sexier outfit that day because he had come to stunt, and she wasn't ready.

"Well, don't you look all churched up, Brishelle. My whole choir lookin' good today!" he said.

Brishelle gave a sly smirk.

"We the best-lookin' choir, if I say so myself. *Carry the Cross* won't know what to do," Mrs. Henderson, the choir member who had been the most helpful to Brishelle, chimed in.

"Who's *Carry the Cross*?" Brishelle said.

"Oh, that's one of the churches coming this afternoon. They always think they can out sing us at our own anniversary every year," AJ whispered.

The choir left the room. Brandon stayed around to put some of the lyrics together but eventually left them alone.

"Well, I guess I better put my robe on," Brishelle said, walking over to the rack with the choir robes.

"You gonna cover all that up?" AJ said with a sly smile.

"Why you so concerned? You should be thinking about your sick wife at home."

AJ cornered his eyes on her breasts and turned around to lock the choir door again.

"Oh, so you wanna finish what you started last time?" Brishelle said almost in a whisper.

"Maybe I do. You won't give me any other time to get to know you. You halfway cussed me out last time you texted me," he said.

"Wow! It's because you knew you were wrong. Trying to make me seem like the bad guy...Jezebel, I guess."

"I never said I don't have any responsibility in this, but you know I can't let this get out in the church."

"Well, what if it did?"

"Let's just hope it won't. I wanna stay married."

"Oh, so I'm your forever side chick?"

"Naw, I didn't say that. I mean, I want to move forward with you, of course. You're the kind of woman I see myself with, but I can't really do that right now at the moment because…"

He hesitated to finish his sentence.

"Because what…you love her more?"

"All right, saints!"

Both of them could hear the pastor shouting down the hall in his usual way to get those who were drinking cold coffee and stale biscuits in the back to join the service.

"Well, let me go on in there and get ready. Text me, love," AJ said after biting his lower lip and winking at her.

He always left whatever cologne he had on in the room behind him, and it always turned Brishelle on. He always left her with this overwhelming feeling of lust. However, AJ saying that he still felt some love for his wife made her angry. She wanted to finally take ownership of his heart. She wanted to be his only woman. She felt as if his wife never deserved his love in the first place. He had a special, tender, and sexy kind of love that should be reserved for only the most beautiful and tender-hearted women. He felt as if he was a waste of a husband by his wife's side.

She tried to calm down those dark, evil thoughts in her mind, but she couldn't help how she felt about him. All of a sudden, she felt the closest she had ever been to getting to be with the man of her dreams, and she would go to great lengths to get him. She didn't feel as if she'd be breaking up a happy home anyway; he said it himself, Tasha wasn't his type.

Brishelle put on her choir robe and headed down the hall into the sanctuary to join the rest of the choir. Brandon led the choir through all three of their songs effortlessly. Her pretty soprano harmonized perfectly with the choir. She even felt as if the choir members were a lot warmer to her since Tasha wasn't there.

After the choir sat down, Bishop Loving stood up to begin his sermon of the morning. He was wearing a simple black suit and a red tie. Like most pastors, he would probably change into something different for the anniversary service. The pastor and wife usually matched every year for the service. His wife wore a rather understated church suit as well. Brishelle figured she was getting ready to show off this evening, so she wouldn't do too much holy stunting this morning.

There were fewer members than usual in the audience. Brishelle assumed they were probably in the church's kitchen, making the anniversary dinner and that extra sugary, diabetes-inducing Kool-Aid. Brishelle planned to go and get her own dinner somewhere else. She hated all that greasy food the old ladies in the church made.

She also hated eating random people's cooking who didn't work in a temperature controlled fast food kitchen.

The pastor began his message by getting straight to the point.

"Now I want y'all to go with me to Hebrews 13:4. Read the book, somebody!"

A woman who looked to be about 400 pounds in an ill-fitted black dress stood up with her bible.

"The word says, 'Marriage should be honored by all and the marriage bed be kept pure, for God will judge the adulterer and all the sexually immoral."

"Judge who?" the pastor shrieked.

"The adulterer and the sexually immoral, sir."

"Now turn to Proverbs 6:32 somebody."

The same woman remained standing and quickly glided over to the other chapter.

"It reads… But a man who commits adultery has no sense; whoever does so destroys himself."

Brishelle could feel her heart beat in her throat. She immediately felt convicted but tried her best to look as innocent as possible. She nodded in agreement.

"Now, church!" The pastor's voice boomed throughout the pews. "Now y'all know better than to be living an adulterous life out here. You going straight to hell!"

The crowd roared with individuals shouting, "Preach, Preacha!" and "Say that, Bishop!"

Brishelle clapped her hands in agreement. She knew adultery was wrong, but technically, she wasn't committing adultery because she and AJ had never officially had sex.

Brishelle tried to look over at AJ during the sermon, but she didn't want to make anything obvious. She wondered if the pastor had heard she and AJ talking. She thought that was very unlikely, but this was a small church, and people talked. AJ looked like the type to talk too much, Brishelle thought.

The bishop continued preaching at length about sexual sins, including fornication and homosexuality. He only briefly touched on those topics and seemed to make the main message about adultery. It also seemed as if the message was geared toward mistresses as opposed to the men who were cheating on their wives.

"These Jezebels sometimes be in the church," the pastor crooned. "But I know somebody who can save a soul!"

The pastor was beginning to sing-preach as pastors usually do when they were getting toward the end of their morning message. AJ played the organ right behind them. He was "backing him up" as they say. This is when the preacher begins to preach to a tune, and the organ encourages the audience to become livelier by cheering on the pastor. The organ was like the church cheerleader. It was up to the organ whether you danced through the aisles or sang a somber hymn.

Brishelle felt it was safe enough to look back toward the organ where AJ was seated. The pastor had finished most of his rebukes of adulterers, so she felt it was safer to make eye contact.

She tried to get eye contact with him, but he was too busy following the pastor and looking at the other musicians.

During the altar call, Brishelle thought she would sneak out and put her robe up. She felt that she should probably start working on her songs for this afternoon anyway. As she lifted her index finger to glide past the other sopranos in the section who were now busy on their phones, AJ finally caught eye contact with her.

"Where you goin'?" AJ whispered.

"Getting something to eat. I'll be back," she whispered back.

She quickly walked down the steps and placed her robe back on the rack in the choir room.

"You ready to sing tonight?" Brandon said.

He almost startled her. He was sitting on one of the couches in the choir room, eating Chinese food with his tie off.

"Yeah, I'm 'bout to get something to eat now. I see you already have."

"Girl, yes! I was hungry. I don't like all that food they cook anyway."

"Well, I'll try and practice those songs while I'm on my way there. I wouldn't want to embarrass the person who was originally supposed to sing when she hears about it."

"Oh, Tasha? She'll be here. She just had to miss the main service, but you're still taking her place."

Brishelle was not ready to sing in front of her while she sat in the audience. She had a difficult time as it was sitting next to her.

When Brishelle came back from getting lunch, she noticed the parking lot was almost full.

She suddenly decided to check her phone, and she had missed a text from AJ.

Where were you going to eat? He had texted her.

I already came back. Wyd?

He replied almost immediately.

Damn…replied all extra late AND didn't get me no food. Damn, babe.

Who's babe?

He sent an emoji face that had the tongue playfully sticking out.

She always hated when people didn't just say what they meant.

Come to the choir room, he texted.

She left her leftover food in the car, then walked over to the choir room.

There was no one in there. Everybody else in the choir was in the dining room, "whooping and hollering" as her mother would have said.

They immediately locked eyes when she walked in.

"Come sit next to me."

He patted the couch on the opposite side of him to motion for her to come over. She hesitated because anyone could walk in at any time, but she rarely spent time with him, so she decided she would go ahead and take the chance.

As soon as she sat down, he touched his leg with hers and placed his hand on her thigh. He sent shivers down her spine almost immediately. She had closed the door behind her, but it wasn't locked. However, the possibility of getting caught turned her on a little bit. She pressed his face against hers and sucked on his mouth like she was trying to get oxygen. Her nipples hardened, and she grabbed his hard dick while pushing him on his back. He placed two fingers inside her and began thrusting. She became wetter than a waterfall and moaned in his ear as softly as she could. She wanted him now, and she was finally about to receive what she had been craving.

Heavy footsteps began to trail towards the door. They jumped off each other immediately. Brishelle almost ran to the other side of the room to pretend she was on her phone. AJ decided to act as if he had been taking a nap.

"Hey, son!" Bishop Loving said. "You ready to play me some of that sweet, heavenly music?"

"I'm ready, Bishop! Just trying to get a nap in before I tear that organ up!"

"Well, all right, son. I'm looking forward to it!"

Bishop Loving turned around to go change into his anniversary suit and the dining room talk seemed to mellow down as it neared 3:30.

"Well, I'm gonna go and practice in the car a little bit," Brishelle said to AJ.

"You gonna leave me here all horny and shit?"

"Shhhh…we are still in church." Brishelle tried to quiet him down.

"Yeah, and we almost smashed in church."

"Well, I'm going to the car. I'll text you…babe," she winked.

On her way to the car, he sent her about eight kiss face emojis in a row. She was beginning to like him more and more. He was everything she had ever needed and wanted. He made her feel more alive. She felt like she finally had a man, although he wasn't officially her man yet. She prayed he would be, though.

When the service began, the pastor and wife did a slow march down the aisle, holding onto the arms of the highest church officials, which were the assistant pastor and his wife.

Brishelle sang "Give Me My Flowers" in her melodic voice. She put her own spin on it, but she could tell the crowd enjoyed it.

She saw Tasha in the crowd, trying not to pay attention to her. She didn't even stand for the processional. Everyone usually stood until the pastor and wife took their seats. Tasha seemed really pissed off that Brishelle had taken her place. Brishelle didn't care, though, and kept singing as if she didn't exist. She decided to be a little petty towards the end of her song and did a run with her vocals as Tasha usually did. Tasha immediately looked up and rolled her eyes.

Brishelle looked back at AJ, who had his usual Kool-Aid smile on his face.

The choir stood up to sing their first selection for the evening. Tasha delivered the first verse of "Great Is

Your Mercy" and the people almost stood up immediately. Tasha sat towards the back, pretending to read the anniversary service's program. After the choir sang, Brishelle watched AJ get off the organ and sit next to his wife. He gave her a light kiss on the forehead and lightly rubbed her thigh. He then put his arm around her to watch the rest of the service. The remainder of the anniversary service would include long-winded speeches and poorly written poems dedicated to the pastor and his wife.

Brishelle left service early because she was tired, and also because she couldn't stand to see AJ all hugged up with his wife when he knew he was only doing that to make a point to everyone that he was happily married. She almost felt sorry for him that he was trying to keep up appearance in a loveless marriage.

Brishelle went home, but this time, she felt pretty good. She kind of had a boyfriend again. She decided she would just claim it. She felt that eventually, something would happen, and she would get to have him all to herself.

When she got home, she expected to get a text from AJ, but she didn't. She found it strange, but she assumed he was still busy with church or his wife. She never liked to text first, but she decided that since they were a lot more comfortable with each other now, they could.

She had his name saved under "Zaddy" in her phone. She knew he couldn't have possibly put her actual name in his phone, so she figured maybe she was under "Pizza" or something.

She texted him around nine.

WYD?

She felt that was enough to get her point across. She would just wait for him to reply with some flirtatious emoji.

After about an hour, he hadn't texted her back yet. She began to get worried, but she also realized that she was technically the side chick, so he had to see about his main family first before he talked to her.

Brishelle went to bed around midnight, and AJ still hadn't texted her back. She was irritated, but she would leave it alone until the morning.

Brishelle immediately looked at her phone when she got up in the morning. He had his read receipts on, so he had seen her text but never responded. Brishelle was enraged. How dare he ignore her like that. She decided to send him a text to outline her frustration in ten words or less.

Oh, so it's like that? Whatever. She then sent an emoji that was rolling its eyes.

Whenever she ended a sentence with a period, she was officially pissed off.

AJ responded within five minutes.

Damn, bae! Mad at me again? LOL! I saw your text but forgot to respond. My nephew stayed overnight, so I got busy with that and my wife is still sick...so yeah.

It seemed somewhat believable, but she was still a little pissed. Brishelle decided to send a text back about an hour later.

Oh, I just got this…sorry.

I *see what you doin', babe. Lol, he replied.* **You still gonna make it to the picnic…since I assume that's the next time I'll see you.**

Yeah…I plan on going, she quickly texted back.

What you gon' wear? he replied.

Clothes…lol.

Me too…that sounds sexy…

LOL, OK, baby. Well, I'll let you get back to your busy life, Brishelle replied.

My life always includes you, baby.

Brishelle had to stop and look at the text for a few seconds. A wave of love came over her. She had never been texted something so sweet in her life. She took a screenshot of the text to keep it. It really felt like he meant what he said. There was no doubt in her mind that he possibly loved her or at least strongly liked her. She wanted to see him before the picnic.

Well, maybe we could meet up on Friday night, she texted.

Naw, me and the wife goin' over her mom's house for her dad's birthday.

Well, what day works for you? she asked.

Ummm, I'm not sure... I'm real busy this week, he replied.

Brishelle rolled her eyes and became angry all over again. This side chick life had a lot of drawbacks, but she was willing to roll with the punches.

Oh... I thought your life ALWAYS included me. You were lying?

Baby, you are in my life, but I just can't get up and go when I want. I'm not single like you. I'm single in my heart because I want only you, but baby, you know my situation.

She sighed and accepted it. She wanted him so bad that even half a man was better than none at all. No one had ever made her feel like AJ had. He was one of a kind. She was willing to risk it all as long as he was.

Saturday arrived, and Brishelle was mentally and physically ready to finally see AJ outside of the confines of the church. It was a picnic so she couldn't get too sexy, but she wanted to show him her casual-cute self.

She texted him, *Can't wait to see you.*

She got dressed and put her hair in a cute bun towards the back with a few hairs purposely hanging out. She put on a full face of makeup, but with more muted colors, so she didn't look like she was trying too hard. She wore a tight t-shirt and jeans that hugged every curve God had given her. The t-shirt had a V-neck that scooped down to give a peak of her DD cup breasts. She made sure she wore a matching bra and panty set. She wore a pair of comfortable flats and a long, burgundy duster cardigan. She was classy with a little sex appeal. She had a pretty face anyway, so she didn't have to try as hard as most women. Her chocolate complexion glowed, and she made sure she put a little gold highlight on those high cheekbones of hers.

When she arrived at the picnic, most of the church was already there. The older women, who apparently weren't used to dressing casually, had on large t-shirts with the church's name emblazoned on the front and long, jean material, ankle-length skirts. She wondered how they were all able to find the same atrocious jean skirt.

She parked her car and then walked over to the area where the church was seated. She brought her portable chair and a blanket.

Brandon waved her down so she could sit with the choir.

"Honey! We all over here, girl!"

Brishelle quickly looked around but carried her stuff over to the choir's section of the park.

AJ was sitting with his wife, eating some chips. His wife was talking to Kimiesha and Tyanna on her blanket.

She tried to make a quiet entrance, but AJ welcomed her before she could sit down.

"Well, welcome, soprano! I guess we all here now!"

Tasha looked back, but then turned right back around to keep talking as if she wasn't even there.

Brishelle found a seat as far away from AJ as possible without seeming too antisocial against the choir.

She noticed several attempts by Tasha to make sure that everyone knew AJ was hers. She sat on his lap, she stroked his face, and even made sure she got his plate.

One of the other choir members even shouted out, calling them, "The cutest couple ever!"

Brishelle mentally rolled her eyes. She smiled and looked approvingly at them. She then uttered, "AJ's a very lucky man."

AJ then looked lovingly at his wife and kissed her on the lips. "I sure am!"

Brishelle could feel the deceptiveness in those words in her heart.

Most of the food was prepared, so the older people, including the pastor and wife, began to eat first.

The young people, including AJ, decided to go on the short hike up the hill. Although Brishelle had on flats, she decided that she'd go halfway, and then come back down.

A few young children came along, including a few of AJ's nieces and nephews. He seemed to love children, which made Brishelle's heart fill up even more whenever she looked at him. She tried not to walk too closely. She then got a text.

I see your sexy ass behind me.

She could have screamed with delight.

Yeah…just don't walk too fast, she replied.

AJ and the children were about fifteen feet ahead of her. There were a few other choir members younger than twenty-five who had come along as well. Brandon had also decided to make the short trip with them.

About twenty minutes into the hike, which consisted of a long, windy trail, Brishelle decided to stop and sit in one of the gazebos alone and enjoy her natural surroundings.

The kids ran back off to their parents when the food was ready, but AJ walked back down the trail to see Brishelle sitting by herself.

"Why you alone?" he said with his deep, velvety voice.

"I just wanted to rest here and soak in the natural surroundings, that's all."

"I bet that's not all you gonna soak in." AJ put his hands on her thighs and rubbed them.

They forgot all about who might catch them or who would see. At this point, they just wanted each other, despite all the obstacles that could come against them. This was the first time he had shown public affection for her. They were all the way across the park where the other churches were located, but the gazebo was hidden enough from plain sight, so they felt safe enough to get close to each other.

They kissed, talked, and caressed each other. This was the first time she heard, 'I love you' leave his lips. This 'relationship' was moving a little fast for her, but it felt right. It felt like this was the man God had sent to her.

About twenty minutes later, they decided to go back to the main picnic area where the rest of the church was. They decided to let one or the other go first so they wouldn't come back to the picnic at the same time. Brishelle decided to go first so she could get something to eat. She was starving.

While walking back to one of the picnic tables after she got her food, Brishelle noticed Tasha talking to AJ. She looked angry. She was pointing at his face, and almost looked like she wanted to push him. They were standing next to the women's restroom, and they were loud enough for anyone who walked by to hear them. The older people were further away from the picnic table so they wouldn't have been able to see or hear them.

He looked like he was trying to explain himself and calm her down. The last thing Brishelle heard was a loud, "Whatever, nigga," from Tasha.

Brishelle's heart dropped. She knew that their argument possibly had to do with her.

She decided to text AJ.

So…what happened?

Somebody saw us over there talking, he responded.

They saw us kiss?

*Naw…I don't think so…but she's really trippin'
over nothin'. She's annoying.*

Brishelle was somewhat relieved, but still
embarrassed.

She decided to eat with some of the older women at
the picnic table. She wanted to get up and leave, but she
thought it would look too obvious. She tried to smile with
the older women and eat her food in peace.

As the picnic ended, she noticed the church
members beginning to pack up their chairs and to-go plates.
Brishelle decided it was time for her to leave, too, so she
sent him a message.

I'm getting ready to go…see you a little later.

He didn't respond as quickly as she had hoped.

While she was getting ready to walk over to her car, she noticed AJ and his wife praying. He then loudly began exclaiming how much of a "jewel" she was to anyone who was in earshot. He told the rest of the choir that everybody goes through something, but that he loved his wife to pieces.

AJ went on.

"Baby, I didn't do nothing with that woman. I don't know her like that. She don't got nothing on my baby."

That cut right through Brishelle's heart like a knife.

She hated how he always calmed Tasha down just to make her feel better about herself.

A part of her still wanted him. He was her heart, even if he couldn't express it publicly. When they kissed inside the gazebo, she saw sparks fly everywhere. That was real love to her, and she wasn't going to let that go so easily. Wife or no wife.

Suddenly, a text from AJ popped up on her phone.

Hey, wanna meet up tonight?

Chapter Seven
Secret Lovers

Brishelle put on the sexiest dress she owned. It fit her booty and breasts so well, it was as if she wasn't wearing anything at all. It was a bodycon dress that hugged every crevice of her God-given, gorgeous body. Her dress came down just below her booty. She wore her hair even longer this time, so it touched her lower back. She had just gotten new bundles shipped to her this weekend, so she was able to easily clip them in herself for instant length and thickness. She made sure she smelled amazing, wearing her favorite Marc Jacobs fragrance. This was possibly the most special night to wear it.

You still picking me up?

Yeah, I'm on the way.

Brishelle and AJ were headed on their first date together. His wife was on vacation with her sorority sisters, so they thought it was the perfect week to get much-needed quality time together.

He texted her that he was there.

She took one last look in the mirror to make sure everything was perfect. She looked and felt the sexiest she'd ever been.

He pulled up to her driveway and texted her that he was there. She walked out in her six-inch heels with the curls in her hair bouncing with each step. She made sure she brought extra makeup in her bag just in case he ruined it a little bit. She hoped he would.

He was in a black, 2018 Mercedes CLS Class. It looked brand new as if he had just rolled it out of the Mercedes' dealership.

He got out of the car to open the door for her. He kissed her lightly on the lips and tightly put his arms around her waist.

"Damn...you lookin' good as hell. Come here and let me bite that."

She put one of her fingers to his lips.

"Why don't we wait until the date has gone on at least fifteen minutes before you start doing too much," she said with a sly smile.

"I'm sorry, baby. You just look so fuckin' good, I'm ready to take you to the house right now."

She got in the car, and he shut the door behind her. He had Marvin Gaye playing in the background. He got in the driver's seat and checked her out one more time and bit his bottom lip before he began to drive off. Brishelle hadn't been in a Mercedes with a man this fine in a long time.

"Oh, so you decided to play those old school, baby making songs?"

"Yeah, just a little something to set the mood."

"Who told you anything was happening tonight? I never said I wanted to go back to your house, did I?"

"Baby, we're adults. There's a lot of sexual tension in this car, and I know you want it just as bad as I do. Don't sit up here and pretend."

Brishelle decided not to say anything. He was right. She wasn't fooling anyone. She was going to finally get more than the tip this time.

They arrived at the swanky Beverly Hills restaurant around seven p.m. It was a Saturday night, and the L.A. streets were crawling with heavy traffic. He stopped in front of the valet and got a ticket to drop his car off.

Brishelle felt like a celebrity. All she needed were paparazzi cameras flashing in her face, trying to see who she was.

The valet was about to help her out of the car, but AJ swooped in to grab her hand, and instead, gave him the keys. The valet nodded and went to the other side of the car to drive it away.

"Two for Sterling," AJ said.

Brishelle began to imagine her name as Brishelle Sterling, and going everywhere together as the "Sterlings". The hostess led them directly to their table without hesitation. AJ made sure he followed Brishelle as she followed the hostess. They sat down at the cozy table for two with a single candle that was lit.

AJ pulled out her seat, then walked to the other side of the table to sit down.

"You're such a gentleman, AJ. I didn't think they made 'em anymore."

"Oh, you mean pulling out your chair? That's what a man is supposed to do. I take care of my woman in more ways than one. I wouldn't ever want to see you struggle to do nothing...except to put on a pair of jeans...that is."

His wide eyes narrowed as he smiled.

Brishelle was caught in them and couldn't stop staring. She couldn't believe what she had in front of her.

"I love you, AJ, and you treat me so well, but I just wish this could be official, you know?"

"Like what?"

"Like being a couple."

"We are a couple, babe. You my girl."

Brishelle playfully rolled her eyes.

"You know what I mean. I guess you're my boyfriend."

"Yeah, I am…and you're my girl."

"You just can't claim me," Brishelle said.

"Well, not right now because of my situation, but baby, that's gonna change one of these days. You just gotta be patient."

"Well, how patient?"

"Look," AJ started. "I'm not trying to get into all this right now. I'm trying to have a beautiful night with my baby. You know what they say; what's understood doesn't have to be explained."

Brishelle knew that social media quote very well. It was the side chick code of honor, she just never thought she'd be living by that saying.

Brishelle changed the topic.

"So, you seem to do pretty well for yourself. A home, a nice car, a great career...why no kids?"

"Tasha and I don't really want any right now. She's been busy with her career, and we don't have the time right now. But I wanna know why a fine-ass woman such as yourself hasn't been scooped up already."

"Well, according to you, I am scooped up."

"Well, I mean, before me. When was your last relationship?"

"About two years ago. It was a mess. I don't wanna talk your ear off," she said.

"No, I understand. I didn't have the best relationships way back, either."

He put out his hand out to hold hers across the table.

He softly rubbed her hands, and she rubbed his back. She felt as if they were the only ones at the restaurant. She couldn't focus on anything else but reflect on the future she hoped they would have together.

She imagined their life together, which included a little boy or girl who had his glowing, dark skin and straight teeth. She wanted to name the girl Aliyah and the boy Alex so they could have names similar to their father's name, Alfred.

He asked her to pick out anything she wanted on the menu. They both chose the filet mignon with potatoes as a side. She couldn't remember the last time she'd eaten filet mignon. Most of the time, she'd never been able to afford it. She was on a strict, living single in Los Angeles budget.

He bought an expensive wine for the table. Brishelle then eyed the check, and it looked like he had tipped generously. She wondered where he had gotten all this money from. She wondered if he was splurging just for today, or if this was what he did on the daily. She thought his wife must be living like a queen. She then imagined not only the children they would have, but the private school they would go to, and how he'd be able to provide the children with everything her alcoholic father never could.

"You wanna head out, baby?"

She nodded.

They walked out to the valet area, arm in arm. She felt powerful being by the side of such a strong, black man. To her, he looked like he could have been some kind of Nigerian warrior back in the day. She held onto his arm and his muscles. He felt so strong. She couldn't wait for him to toss her on his bed.

Once they were in the car, he played "Between the Sheets" by The Isley Brothers. He then rested his hand on her thigh and pulled her dress up a little bit, so more of her thigh showed. He licked two of his fingers and pressed them against her pussy. He slid his fingers underneath her panties and began rubbing his fingers around in a circle until she got wetter.

Brishelle moaned in ecstasy. She almost shed a tear because it felt so good. At the stoplight, he pulled her face towards his and passionately kissed her. It was one of those sloppy, wet kisses that Brishelle craved. She wanted to jump on his lap right then and there, but she knew they were headed to his house.

As soon as he pulled up to the driveway, she saw that his dick was already hard and pressed against his slacks. She grabbed it, then he placed his hand inside her bra to caress her nipple. He pulled the low neck of her dress down so he could suck on them.

He pulled her by the hand out of the car and shut the door behind her. He opened up the door and picked her up with her legs straddling him, and they drifted into the house.

He took her upstairs to the master bedroom and softly laid her down on the bed. She took off her dress, and he unbuttoned his shirt to remove it. He pulled down his Calvin Klein boxer briefs to reveal his hard dick. He was about eight and a half inches long, and thicker than a Snickers bar. Before she knew it, they were both naked and lying on top of his California King bed.

He immediately began to thrust into her. He went slowly, then picked up the pace. It was better than she could have ever imagined. It was so good, tears began to come down from her eyes. She moaned and screamed his name. She didn't care if his neighbors heard. He tried to quiet her down by forcing her face into the pillow when he began to hit it from the back. She grabbed anything she could as he gave her hard but satisfying pumps.

She had just remembered that they had forgotten to use a condom, but at this point, she just wanted him to keep going and finish. His six-pack dripped sweat as she watched his chest move back and forth as he kept thrusting. After several positions, heavy breathing, and sweat, he finished inside of her.

He rolled over as soon as he was done to catch his breath. They must have been going for about forty-five minutes straight. They were both exhausted. She wanted to cuddle him, but he made a gesture meant to push her off. She then rolled over to the other side of the bed and decided to clean herself up.

When she came back, he was fast asleep. She wondered how someone could go to sleep that quickly. He managed to put himself under the covers and kept his clothes off.
In his ear, she whispered, "I love you."

"Uh-huh," he moaned. His eyes remained closed, and he tried to drift back to sleep.

She figured she would be able to stay the night, so she decided to find one of his t-shirts because she didn't feel like sleeping naked.

She decided that it would be best not to cuddle him for the night as she had hoped. She turned off the lights and drifted off to sleep as well. She was finally satisfied. Her pussy was still wet and felt like it was trying to regain its shape. She could feel some of the cum slowly dripping out of her and onto the t-shirt.

She kissed him goodnight for the last time and slept soundly next to him.

Brishelle got up before AJ in the morning. He was still fast asleep, but she needed to get back home to do some work. She knew she'd have to do the walk of shame in an Uber, but she thought it was worth it. She didn't think it was necessary to wake him up just to drive her home.

She put her dress back on and put her heels on. She wished she had brought some flats with her.

She looked over at him to see him sleeping as soundly as a little baby. He was such a tall and dominant man whose dark skin contrasted so well with the white bed sheet draped across his body.

She removed her heels once again and tiptoed over to him to kiss him on the cheek. His eyes began to open a bit as he tried to wake up.

"You leaving, babe?" AJ said in a sexy, gravelly voice. Brishelle had always loved how men sounded when they first woke up, especially if they already had a very deep voice.

"Yeah, I was gonna head out. I got a lot of work to do."

"You callin' an Uber?"

"Well, I'm gonna have to. You half asleep."

"All right, I'll hit you up later then."

He then closed his eyes and fell back asleep.

Brishelle was somewhat put off by his short and terse response. She expected him to want to spend a little more time with her or at least say "I love you." He seemed satisfied with what he had gotten last night and wanted nothing more.

He had shown so much affection last night, she expected him to be much more loving and tender with her in the morning.

She admitted to herself that he was very tired and would definitely text her later. She couldn't believe that how he behaved last night was just for sex. She could feel he wanted more with her.

A couple of days later, Brishelle received a beautiful bouquet of flowers delivered to her door. They were from AJ. He sent them for no special occasion. The two had been texting and sexting back and forth since their last encounter. His texts were much longer and more detailed. He said "I love you" more often and made a promise to see her that weekend. He told her that he didn't expect his wife to come back until Monday morning.

AJ had definitely become a distraction to her work, and she hadn't been as productive as before. She couldn't stop thinking about him. She felt like a little school girl thinking about her first crush. Brishelle couldn't remember the last time anyone had ever made her feel this way. She spent more time watching romantic-comedies and bought new lingerie just for him. She even began telling people who weren't extremely close to her that she had a boyfriend. She wouldn't dare mention it to her mother or her best friend Tiera because they would eventually find out that it was AJ from probing her with invasive questions.

She even began talking to friends and family far less than she had ever been. She texted and called AJ much more often than anyone else who was close to her. She told him all her secrets and ambitions. She knew more about his past than she had ever known about anyone else.

Choir rehearsal had been canceled this week so she wouldn't see him until Sunday. They were in a group chat with the choir where everyone agreed to sing a couple of older songs they all knew that wouldn't need too much rehearsal.

Brishelle almost couldn't believe that she and AJ had this full-blown relationship and it was a total secret. She bet the choir members would never suspect that she and AJ had been messing around. He had pretended to love his wife so much, he definitely helped to throw them off the scent.

Brishelle finally decided to add AJ on social media. He added her back and followed her on more than one account of hers. She had altered her profile, so it said she was in a relationship, and AJ immediately sent her a winking emoji along with, **I see you, babe!**

Everything about them seemed real. She felt they were truly in love. The only thing that was left was to get AJ to publicly claim her. She knew that would possibly take a while, and she didn't want him to divorce his wife so quickly. She wanted to make it an easy transition, which she felt was doable because he didn't have children yet.

On Monday, AJ's wife Tasha came back to Los Angeles. He told Brishelle this, and she hated seeing that message on her phone. She had been happy to have AJ all to herself for about a week, but she figured that one day, she would have him permanently.

Brishelle decided to take a break from church this Sunday. She had a lot going on with the website, and she wanted to be on standby all day. She had finally hired a lifestyle/romance freelance writer for her website, and she was in the midst of doing more promos for local and black-owned natural hair companies. Business was finally moving in the direction she wanted. Her love life was somewhat in order, too, she just hoped she and AJ could move on with their future perfect lives a lot sooner.

She dreamt of the big suburban home that she and AJ would own and the matching black BMWs. Two successful black people getting married were a match made in heaven. She thought he had just made a mistake with his first wife and would finally come to his senses and be that power couple she knew they both had their eyes set on becoming.

Around two p.m., after church was over, Brishelle decided to text AJ to see what he was up to. She had become comfortable calling him "babe" or "bae" in every text she sent now. He replied, telling her how church had gone and how much he had missed her. She asked when they would see each other again, and he told her he wasn't sure, but he hoped he could this weekend.

Brishelle was used to being put on the back burner by now, but she held on, knowing that soon enough, she'd be his priority. Brishelle asked him if they could see each other Saturday night, but he said he was supposed to be going out with his frat boys that night. She asked for a weekday, but he told her that this week wasn't the best because his wife would be working from home this week, and the likeliness of them getting caught was much higher. He said that he would continue to text her as often as he could and that he would FaceTime her when he got to the office.

Every now and then, Brishelle would feel a slight sense of remorse since she was essentially breaking up someone's home. She wouldn't want anyone to do that to her, but she felt like most women couldn't compete with her. She felt she was better than Tasha in every way. She was more fit, she was better looking, she was more successful, and he even told her that his wife had never been able to tighten up her pussy during the act like she could.

Tiera called Brishelle since she hadn't heard from her in a while.

"Girl, where you been? I ain't heard from you in a minute."

"Yeah, I been busy."

"Who is he?" Tiera said.

Brishelle wanted to keep up the lie that she was single, but part of her wanted to spill everything out to her best friend. She wanted her to know all the details and how much in love she felt, but she knew Tiera would never forgive her if she were sleeping with a married man. She was trying to keep it a secret the best she could.

"It's nobody, Tiera. I've just been busy with work."

"You were busy with work before, and you weren't ignoring me like this. You and AJ been getting closer, huh? Isn't that man married?"

"Wow! I know that! I do not like him like that. We not even that cool. You sitting up here making shit up."

"I'm just saying…you seemed to be obsessed with dude last time we talked."

"Well, I'm not. He's very happily married, and I'm still dating online like I always did," Brishelle lied.

"Oh, so you were really ignoring me just to be ignoring me? Damn. Well, you some kind of best friend."

Girl, I told you I been busy as all hell, damn. I ain't even been talking to my momma like that."

"Mhmmm. OK…well, I'll let you go then. I was just seeing what happened. You haven't ignored me this long since that time I hit you in the face with the tetherball in fifth grade."

Brishelle laughed.

"Yeah, girl, I'm not ignoring you. I'm just a busy woman."

"All right. Love you, Bri."

"Love you, Tee."

Brishelle hated lying to her best friend. She'd lie to her mother before she'd lie to Tiera. She felt bad that Tiera could sense what was going on between her and AJ, but Tiera didn't understand how badly Brishelle wanted a family with a strong, black provider. Tiera would never date a married man, but she also didn't date many men who had a checking account and car that wasn't in the shop.

Brishelle decided to FaceTime AJ. She missed him and wanted to hear his voice for a few minutes before she got back to work. She called him, and he didn't pick up. She assumed he was busy and would call her later. After a few hours, he still hadn't called her back, so she decided to text him. He always made her anxious whenever he didn't answer her call or text within fifteen minutes. She always felt like she was losing his attention. There was always that possibility that he could drop her in an instant and move on with his wife.

Hey, baby...I been busy with work. What's up?

Brishelle's heart always fluttered with joy whenever she saw AJ's name pop up on her phone. It was better than receiving a package in the mail, or even getting her tax money back. She felt as if the whole world stopped when she saw a text come through from him. Almost instantly, all the frustration she felt from him taking so long to text back would disappear.

Nothin', I just wanted to hear from my baby, she replied.

Awww, I miss you, too, my li'l sexy woman. I wanna see you soon, though, I just don't know when.

Brishelle couldn't stand when men couldn't make immediate plans to see her. She always wanted them to drop what they were doing if she was so important to them. She forgave AJ, though. AJ was different. He was successful, brilliant, and handsome. She would wait for him longer than she would wait for anybody.

Brishelle went to choir rehearsal on Thursday. She dressed a little more casual this time with a pair of Jordans and a matching sports sweater. She didn't think she had to try as hard to get his attention anymore.

He encouraged her to lead a song on Sunday while he was on the organ. Tasha still wasn't speaking to her, but at this point, Brishelle didn't mind.

She was asked to lead "I Will Bless The Lord" on Sunday. Brishelle always loved that song and was honored to finally sing lead on Sunday morning. That would be the first song the choir would sing that morning. Tasha would sing "Total Praise" before the pastor preached. Only the pastor's wife and the best singer in the choir were reserved to sing before the pastor's morning message. Brishelle wanted that role soon as just about everything else she coveted about Tasha's life.

On Sunday morning, Brishelle got ready for church. She wore a new, red dress that flared out from her hips. It almost looked like a dress from the 1950s. The short sleeves fell toward her shoulders, and she wore a pearl necklace that gave it a little more vintage flair. She wore a matching red purse with red pumps about four inches tall.

She drove to church listening to old, romance ballads instead of turning on the gospel station. She turned down "Love TKO" by Teddy Pendergrass as soon as she pulled up to the church's parking lot. She was a little late, so the praise team had already started singing.

She decided to trek over the choir stand instead of going into the choir room. She remembered that the choir was not supposed to wear robes today. As she made her way to the choir stand, she decided to sit on the end even though she was supposed to sit by Tasha since she was officially the second soprano in charge.

Brishelle sang the lead during the song "I Will Bless The Lord." As usual, most of the church members stood up when she sang. Tasha finally looked at Brishelle and gave a sly smile. Brishelle's mother "shouted" at the end of the song by running up the aisle and falling out. Even in "the spirit" her mother was overly dramatic, Brishelle thought. However, after singing her song, a sense of shame came over Brishelle. She looked back at AJ, who played the organ as if nothing in the world mattered. He didn't seem to have the least bit of remorse after all they had done. He looked and acted as free as he had before they began to get serious.

Brishelle's heart became heavy. Tears slowly fell from her eyes as she sat back down in the choir stand. The music continued to play at a fast pace, and the mood of the church became very energetic. More people began running down the aisles and even more fell out in the aisles after being prayed over by the pastor and his deacons.

Brishelle stood and lifted her hands to praise God. She began crying heavy tears of remorse for what she and AJ had done. She wanted God to forgive her once again. The pastor prayed over her, and she began to speak in tongues. Brishelle had no idea what had come over her, but she finally wanted to change her life. She didn't want to live with the guilt of being a side chick anymore.

When church ended, she passed right by AJ while he stood in front of the church talking. She would usually greet him with a nod or smile, but this time, she avoided all eye contact with him and quickly walked by.

When she got to her car, she saw AJ's reflection in her side view mirror, looking toward her direction, but she quickly averted her eyes.

An old woman in a wide-brimmed church hat, who looked to be about ninety, shuffled over to Brishelle's car right before she got in.

"Now, baby! You keep on keepin' on for the Lord! The spirit was in ya!"

"Thank you, ma'am."

The old woman smiled and slowly walked back to where the other congregants were talking in the parking lot.

When Brishelle arrived home, she noticed she had two texts from AJ on her phone. She wanted to block him, but he usually told her when choir rehearsal was canceled since the choir director was unreliable.

Hey, love, I saw you walk past me. You too holy for a nigga now? LOL.

She rolled her eyes at the text but decided to reply anyway. She said to herself that this would be the last time she would talk to him. She wanted to move on with her life. She got right to the point.

AJ, I don't think we should see each other anymore. I can't sit up here and be your side chick anymore. I need my own husband someday, and this is not it. It's tearing me up inside, and I think it's time we just let it go.

He responded immediately.

Baby...I'm sorry you feel that way, but I wasn't trying to ruin your life at all. I love you so much, and you've been my whole world ever since I met you. However, if that's how you feel, then we'll just go back to being friends then.

Brishelle was surprised that he had taken the news so well. Part of her wanted him to beg her to stay. However, she knew that this was the right choice. It was time for her to permanently move on. It hurt her because AJ was the most handsome and passionate man she had ever met. She knew she would never meet another, but she felt it wasn't worth an eternity in damnation.

Chapter Eight
What Goes Up Must Come Down

Brishelle was up late, editing an article she wanted to post this week. She wanted to include more celebrity gossip to attract more readers since it seemed to be working for everyone else she knew who owned an online magazine. Since the Sunday service, she buried herself in both work and prayer. She had finally forgiven herself for what she had done with AJ. She felt that hopefully, one day, she could apologize to Tasha.

However, the pain in her heart of possibly never having a man like AJ in her life again wouldn't completely go away. She figured it would take more time to finally get over him. She hadn't blocked his calls or texts yet, but she had put their text thread on silent, so she wouldn't feel compelled to answer. He hadn't texted her in a while anyway. She thought that maybe they both could finally move on.

She decided to go for a jog around her neighborhood before it got too dark. When she picked up her phone to choose her exercise playlist, she saw her text message app was highlighted with a message she had received. She never heard any alert from her phone, and her phone wasn't on vibrate. She instantly knew it was AJ.

Baby…I really miss you. I want to move forward with you. I want you to be my wife, mother of my kids…everything.

Brishelle must have stared at her phone for about five minutes straight before she responded. She had wanted to hear those words her whole life. She didn't want to be anyone's mistress anymore. She was serious about changing her life, but if that included a husband in the future, she wanted to do it.

She wondered if AJ was serious, but at this point, she didn't care because she could always take a screenshot of the message and hold it against him.

Maybe you should come over here and tell me face to face if you mean what you say. I'm not trying to play any games, she replied.

I'm not playing any games. I promise, baby. I'ma come by and see you right now. I'm 'bout to get off work.

When will you be here?

In like 25 minutes or less. I'm not that far away.

Brishelle closed out the work she was doing on the computer and decided to take another shower. She wanted to put on something more fashionable since she was wearing sweats and a big t-shirt. She mentally promised that they wouldn't have sex and she would try to get him to stay in the living room area only. She wanted to have an open and honest conversation about the future of their relationship.

Brishelle played soft, jazz music in the background from her speakers in her living room and sprayed the room down with air freshener. She straightened up the room a little bit and brushed out her hair, so it neatly fell around her shoulders. She had just gotten a new weave installed that fell closer to her armpits this time. She put on a little makeup but decided not to put on any lipstick. She rubbed Vaseline on her lips to soften them just in case they shared a kiss.

About thirty minutes later, she heard AJ's car pull up to the curb, right in front of her apartment. She peered out the window, and he looked like he was trying to search for parking. She took one last look at herself and breathed deeply. She was nervous, and her heart was beating quickly. She hadn't seen him in a while, so a slight twinge of excitement came over her as well.

What's your apartment number? he texted.

I'll come outside. I see you.

Brishelle walked down the stairs, which led directly outside. He stood on the part of the sidewalk nearest to her apartment. He gave her a huge smile as soon as he saw her. Brishelle had her arms open for a hug. He took her and hugged her around her waist so tightly, she could barely breathe for a few seconds.

"You love to give them deadly bear bugs," she joked.

"I missed my baby, so I can't help it."

"Well, come with me upstairs."

He followed behind her. Brishelle couldn't stop thinking that the man right behind her could possibly be her husband or the future father of her children.

"Your place is beautiful. You got it fixed up in here nice," he said as he quickly scanned her large living room space.

"You can have a seat on the couch. Would you like some water?"

"I'm good...have a seat next to me."

She sat next to him, a few inches away, but he reached his arm over her side and pulled her in closer, so their thighs touched.

"Damn...you fine as hell," he said as he stared deeply into her chestnut brown eyes.

"I want to get right to the point, Alfred."

"Damn, calling me by my government and everything. Chill, ma."

"When are you going to leave your wife for me? I need to know now, today, this minute. I'm tired of beating around the bush. I want you, and I know you're the man for me. It hurts that I can't have you when I want you and that I have to sneak around."

"I can see me making some changes in the next six months."

"What changes?"

She looked at him earnestly as if he had the key to open a vault with millions of dollars inside.

"Don't worry about it. It'll happen...now come here."

He tried to pull her face closer to his to kiss her, but she brushed him away with her hand.

"I'm serious, AJ! I'm not your side bitch, sister-wife, none of that shit! You need to claim me. You know our relationship is what you want. You said it yourself."

"Yeah, I do want you, but I just can't up and leave right this minute. I have a lot of ties to her family and shit. It's not that easy, but baby, I'm trying. You don't understand."

"No! You don't understand!" Brishelle snapped.

"Baby, stop all this screaming. You know I love you, and I see us having a future, but we can't move this fast."

"Give me a plan. God wants us together. I can feel it."

"Why you putting God in this now? I mean, damn. Look, Brishelle, I'll tell her I'm in love with you next week on Monday. I'll see how she reacts. It's not gonna be a good reaction, but if she wants to leave, then that's the green light for us. I'm sure she'll file for divorce."

"You promise?"

"I promise, baby. I really wanna be with you, and it's gonna happen. Now come here."

AJ pulled her close to him and kissed her passionately. He lightly pushed her toward the couch, so she was on her back, and began putting his hands under her shirt. She unbuttoned his work shirt and unbuckled his Ferragamo belt. He unsnapped her bra with one hand and began sucking her breasts as if he were trying to suck milk out of them. She dug her nails into his back and suddenly felt him slide his dick inside her. While he was inside, she watched his booty pump up and down as he gave her the whole eight inches.

She moaned as loud as she could and kept shouting "Daddy!" over and over again. He kept grunting as he thrust, and this made her even wetter. Their deep breathing began to synchronize, and he began to move in and out of her even faster. Brishelle threw her head back in ecstasy and bit the pillow on her couch. She clutched his shoulders tightly and kept telling him, "Don't stop."

AJ's phone rang loudly from his jeans. He reached to get it while still inside Brishelle.

"What are you doing?" she blurted, trying to keep his hand away from reaching the phone.

"It's my wife. She gets suspicious if I don't answer it around this time. Hold on."

He put his finger to her lips and answered the call.

Brishelle could hear Tasha clearly on the other end.

"Where are you?" Tasha said in a condescending tone. "Why you breathing so heavy?"

"I'm at the gym."

"When you coming home? I thought we were going to Kendra's little get-together tonight."

"Yeah, we are, baby," he replied. "I was just about to head home anyway."

"All right, bye." Tasha hung up the phone abruptly.

He hung up and proceeded to pull up his pants.

"So, that's it? You not gonna finish?"

"I don't have time, baby. I promised my wife I was supposed to go to this event. I'll come back after, I promise."

He quickly buttoned his shirt, but then asked, "You mind if I take a shower over here?"

She nodded.

He took his clothes upstairs and showered for about ten minutes.

Brishelle was steady trying to put herself back together. She was glad she hadn't put on too much makeup. She wouldn't have wanted to get it on her brand new couch.

After he got out of the shower, he had his shirt and pants on but tucked his button-down shirt under his arm. He put his shoes on and headed out the door.

He told her to come over and kiss him before he left.

She did.

She tried to ask him to stay a little longer, but he shook his head and headed over to his car.

He said, "I'll text you, babe." He then jumped in his Mercedes and pulled off in a hurry.

Brishelle didn't know what to say or think. She felt confused and still unsure of where she and AJ stood.

Baby, will I see you tonight? Brishelle sent a text to AJ within two minutes of him leaving.

I don't know, sweetie. But, ummm… my wife found the receipt from our dinner at Beverly Hills Steakhouse in my coat pocket.

Brishelle was stunned, but part of her hoped this would move Tasha into leaving AJ.

She just hoped Tasha didn't know it was her.

What did she say? Brishelle hesitantly texted back.

She just asked who I took out to dinner and I told her I took Bishop Loving out for his recent retirement.

Did she believe it?

Naw...I don't think so. We argued about it for a while, but she eventually left it alone.

Brishelle took some time to text him back.

About fifteen minutes later, she texted, **I love you.**

A small message that said he had read it appeared under her text. She cried on the couch until she was inconsolable. She was in love with a married man, and every time she tried to break away, he came back to ruin her life once again.

On Sunday morning, Brishelle prepared to go to church. She had been depressed most of the week since AJ never texted her back after the last time they saw each other. She put on her favorite red dress that flared out at the hips, but for some reason, it didn't fit as well as it used to. She decided to wear a white dress she had that was partially made of spandex. She headed out the door and wanted to text AJ, but she decided against it. If he was going to pretend to ignore her, she would, too.

Brishelle arrived at the service around 10:45. She went into the choir room to find her robe. The other choir members were in the church's dining room, eating snacks, so she was the only one in there. AJ walked into the choir room a couple minutes later as Brishelle was buttoning up her choir robe.

She looked at him, but he didn't look back. He grabbed the music lyrics on the table and left out of the choir room quickly.

Brishelle suddenly stopped buttoning her robe and tried to catch up to AJ.

"I need to talk you!" she said in a loud whisper.

"What?"

"OK, so you ignoring me?"

He turned around quickly and went back into the choir room and shut the door behind him.

"Look, I'm trying to make this easy for us. You know I love you, but my wife is starting to get suspicious. She tried to get in my phone last night, and when I wouldn't let her, she cussed me out. I've been living in hell ever since we started this shit. I'm trying to get back to the place where it's a secret."

"I'm not a secret!" Brishelle said in a hushed tone.

"Well, you won't be if we keep this up in public. Give me some time to get her off my ass. I'm gonna move forward with you, but you not making this easy."

"I need to see you, AJ, and I don't care who sees us anymore. You claim to love me. If you do, then you'd try to do everything you could to be with just me. You know you don't love that woman."

"You don't know who the fuck I love!" AJ almost shouted. "My wife is my first priority at the moment. You will be first soon, I promise, but don't make this shit difficult."

He walked out and closed the door behind him, almost slamming it.

Brishelle stood there with a single tear coming down her face. She felt as if AJ was starting to have second thoughts about her. He seemed so confident about leaving his wife for her, but now he was calling Tasha his "priority".

She thought that if Tasha was such a "priority," he wouldn't be messing around with her.

Tasha reluctantly went into the church with her robe on. She drifted into the soprano section where she usually sat. AJ was warming up on the keyboard, waiting for the praise service to start. He seemed to almost intentionally look the other direction. Brishelle wanted to text him a piece of her mind, but she figured she had already sinned enough in church for the day.

Praise service began, and Tasha sang with two younger choir members who were also part of the youth choir.

She sang so loudly, she almost didn't need a mic. The pastor, who typically enjoyed Brishelle when she sang, motioned for her to join the praise team. Brishelle shook her head politely and smiled. The pastor didn't take no for an answer and walked over to AJ and asked him to tell Brishelle to sing with the praise service.

AJ looked at Brishelle without any emotion in his eyes but smiled at the pastor and nodded. He pointed his finger at Brishelle and asked her to come and sing.

Brishelle joined Tasha, who took one look at Brishelle and kept singing as if she didn't exist. Brishelle looked at AJ, who had his head focused on the keys. He never focused on the keys, so he almost looked as if he was guilty of something.

Brishelle knew that Tasha must know what went on between them by now.

Tasha put the mic back on the mic stand when she was done singing. Brishelle attempted to put the mic in her hand to sing, but then AJ sang instead, which appeared to be an effort to silence her.

God is a good God!
(Yes he is!)
Oh I know God is a good God!
(Yes he is!)

Brishelle knew what he was doing and took the lead on the song as soon as she heard a pause.

I know God—

Tasha then sang over her.

Is an awesome God

Brishelle was humiliated. She had never been so embarrassed in her life, and she was sure that some members of the audience could probably tell she wasn't being given her turn to sing. Brishelle decided to play it cool and not sing for the rest of the praise service. She clapped her hands and tried not to let the tear that rested in her tear duct roll down her face.

When praise service was over, Brishelle grabbed her purse and went back to the choir room. She put her robe back on the rack in the choir room. Brishelle saw Brandon rearranging the lyrics inside the desk in the choir room and eating chips.

"I'll see you next Sunday," she said.

Brandon looked at her and then looked back at the lyrics on the desk. He didn't say anything to her. Brishelle felt that was weird of Brandon since he was usually very talkative.

She walked back to her car, and she saw two eleven-year-old girls, who were supposed to be inside, talking and giggling. Brishelle smiled at them. They giggled and turned their heads away quickly. One of the girls, who considered herself the most outspoken of the bunch, ran up to Brishelle.

She looked like she wanted to ask her a question.

"Yes?" Brishelle said.

"Do you like AJ?"

The girl giggled and ran back to laugh with the other little girl. Both girls ran back inside the front opening of the church before Brishelle could say anything.

Brishelle was confused. She wondered how two random little girls in the church would ask whether or not she liked AJ. She rarely looked at AJ in church lately. Her heart dropped in her chest. Not only did she think Tasha knew, but Tasha had also probably told all her closest friends in the church, who then gossiped to everyone else.

Glory Harvest Church of God in Christ was small with only seventy-five to eighty members who made it to service regularly. Brishelle knew gossip spread like wildfire throughout the church. She knew that if those girls knew, then the entire church knew, and she was attempting to sing a praise song with them with everyone looking on. She thought about how awkward it was for her singing to be cut off by Tasha while trying to take the lead.

AJ seemed to have taken Tasha's side now, and she wondered what had caused his change of heart. He had expressed such a deep and passionate love for her, but it seemed like all of that was beginning to fall apart.

Brishelle pulled off from the church's parking lot and rushed home. She immediately took off her heels once inside and put on a pair of comfortable shorts and a t-shirt. She wanted to relax for a bit before she went off on AJ through text. She thought clearly about how this relationship was ruining her life. She wished she could start over again. She would have never gotten so deeply involved with him in the first place. She enjoyed the sex, but the attachments that he had were officially too much to handle. She had ruined her reputation in the church, and couldn't see herself going back there ever again. She knew it was only a matter of time before close friends and family found out.

Brishelle reached for her phone to send her final text to AJ. She didn't care if he didn't respond or not, she just wanted to air out her grievances. She felt he had wasted her time and told her promises he knew he wouldn't be able to keep. She had so much hope for their future, but he never made any effort to make Brishelle part of his life except as a sex partner.

Brishelle looked at her phone, and her mother had called her twice. It was after church, and she wondered if her mother was possibly trying to ask her to come to an evening service at the church. Then, Brishelle saw that her mother had also left a voice message.

She listened to it.

"Breezy...I need you to call me soon. It's important. I want to ask you something. Call me back as soon as you can."

Her mother rarely left voice messages anymore because she knew Brishelle rarely listened to them. Brishelle was a millennial, so she rarely left or listened to voice messages that didn't have anything to do with her job.

Brishelle breathed deeply. She had a feeling her mother wanted to talk to her about something uncomfortable to hear. She almost wished her mother needed to gossip to her about the death of an obscure family member. However, her gut told her that wasn't the case.

Brishelle called her mother, and she picked up on the first ring.

"Breezy…how everything been going?"

"It's been fine, momma."

"I ain't heard from you in a while, so I was a little concerned. You used to call me at least once a week, and now I barely hear from you."

"Is that what you called me for, momma?" Brishelle was frustrated but relieved that her mother didn't have much to say.

"Now, Breezy...I been hearing some crazy rumors from some of the sisters at church about you. Now I hope they not true because I was getting ready to lose my salvation and cuss those devils out."

Brishelle's heart dropped.

"Now, have you and that keyboard player been seeing each other? You know that man's married."

"No, momma! I haven't been with him at all. I know he's married."

"Well, somebody told me they saw you two out to dinner once in Beverly Hills. Deacon Smith is a security guard out that way, and he said he saw you two coming out of a steakhouse. He said the woman looked just like you."

"No, momma! That was not me. He's probably cheating, but not with me. I swear on everything."

"Now, Breezy, I hope you telling the truth because I never known Deacon Smith to lie and start mess. That man never had anything against you, and I never heard him talk about nobody, but AJ is his godson, so he was able to recognize AJ real quick."

Brishelle's heart was almost beating out her chest.

"Well, momma, I don't know what he's talking about because that was not me. AJ is happily married, and I respect that."

"All right, Breezy. Well, I believe you. Don't talk to that man no more at all because if he's cheating on his wife, he ain't no good. He shouldn't be playing God's music in front of the people anyway if he's not saved."

"I know, momma. Well, ummm, I gotta start getting into my work. I need to catch up."

"Well, all right. I'll be talkin' to ya."

"Bye, momma."

Brishelle was stunned. She was beyond embarrassed. She couldn't believe that word had gotten out that quickly around the church. She should have known that, although L.A. was a big city, the Black population was small, and there was a good chance that anybody Black in public might have some connection to her through something.

She hated lying to her mother, but that was the only way to get her off her case. It was not like what she had done was illegal. She had made a terrible mistake, and she would most likely never return to that church again.

Brishelle texted AJ exactly what was on her mind. She didn't want to hold anything back.

I'm officially done with you! You are a fuckin' liar. You never wanted to move forward with me. Now the whole church knows we were together. It was probably you who went around and told. Fuck you and your WHOLE life. Go and be with that fat-ass bitch aka your wife. You lost a really good woman. I'm almost too good for you. You fake-ass Christian. We don't EVER have to see each other again. I'm never coming back to Glory Harvest. Fuck you, the choir, and everything else. Bye.

AJ responded almost immediately.

So, I'm sitting here, trying to have dinner with my family and all of a sudden, I get this vicious-ass text from you. Why are you mad at me? I couldn't promise that I'd leave Tasha for you and you know that. I really fuckin' tried, but it's not that easy. You never been in a relationship longer than two years so you don't know shit. I never put the word out that we were sleeping around, ask Tasha. I heard the Deacon saw us, too. So fuck all this. My reputation is all fucked up now. Tasha is embarrassed and shit. This is all because of you. You the one who begged ME if we could be more public and I did and look what happened. This shit is crazy!

Brishelle was fuming.

Look, nigga! We both got caught and it wasn't either of our faults so don't sit up here and try to blame me. I told you I didn't wanna be no side chick. I wanted us to WORK toward being official and you said you could do that. You were ALWAYS complaining about your wife. You're just a fucking sick individual who wanted to have two women at the same time without consequences.

Brishelle…I'm officially done. Don't fuckin' text me no more. You crazy as fuck. After this text, you're blocked. You out the choir, too. I'll tell Brandon. You on some bullshit. I'm not trying to break my family up for some crazy bitch.

It took everything in Brishelle to not text him anyway. She tried calling him twice, but she couldn't get through. She figured it was because he had blocked her calls and texts.

Brishelle cut off all contact with her family and friends for the next three weeks. She kept a low profile and went to the grocery store and shopped in the white neighborhoods instead, so she wouldn't mistakenly run into anyone who knew her through the church, school, or anywhere else. She assumed that the word had gotten out everywhere.

About two weeks prior, she had received a text message from her friend, Tiera, asking her if she had really been sneaking around with AJ because she had heard some rumors. She said Tasha had made a social media post talking about infidelity and someone mentioned Brishelle's name.

Brishelle never responded and instead blocked her best friend from calling and texting her for the time being. Brishelle deactivated all of her social media accounts and began to slow down on her work. She took a hiatus from the online magazine and promised her readers that she would return by the end of the month. She thought about possibly getting into a new field and moving to another state where no one knew her.

Suddenly, Brishelle began to feel queasy. She figured it was something she had eaten last night that didn't agree with her. She had felt slightly sick the other morning as well. Brishelle's period had recently skipped. She was usually very regular, but her period was supposed to have come on Thursday or Friday and today was Wednesday.

Brishelle assumed the worst and bought a pregnancy test from the store. When she arrived home, she opened the package and went to the bathroom. She bought the most expensive one that revealed a digital message of "pregnant" or "not pregnant" after you peed on it.

Brishelle let the test do its thing for about three minutes. She saw the stick had a digital answer formulated already, but she couldn't read it yet.

Her heart was about to jump out of her chest. She could hear it pumping in her ears.

PREGNANT.

Brishelle almost fell to the floor. She should have known that there was a chance since AJ hadn't pulled out, and she wasn't on birth control. She meant to buy a Plan B package, but she never got the chance. She also thought she wasn't ovulating that day because she didn't feel the cramping she usually felt, so she thought she was safe.

She didn't know who to tell. She had blocked almost everyone out of her life. If she told her mother or best friend, they would ask her so many invasive questions, she would eventually find out that the father was AJ.

She thought about having an abortion, but she didn't believe in it. She wanted to have a baby within the confines of a marriage, but an innocent baby didn't have the choice to decide whether or not they wanted to be here.

She decided she would keep the child and just raise it on her own. She had always wanted a child. She hated that the child would have AJ as a father, but maybe he would eventually help her when she proved that the child was indeed his. This child would be the only piece of AJ she had left. She hated him, but he was still part of her fondest memories. She had yet to meet anyone who had ever treated her the way he had.

She knew she couldn't text or call him to say that she was pregnant. She didn't know what to do, but she knew she would have to tell her mother, who would be the grandmother of the child. Even though her mother would be disappointed, she knew she would eventually come around and help her.

She made good money as the owner of *HeyBlackGrl!*, but she didn't know if she could fully support a child on her own.

Brishelle unblocked her mother's number and called her.

Hello? Brishelle?"

"Momma, I'm pregnant."

There was a long, dramatic pause before her mother could speak.

"By who?"

"The keyboardist at church…AJ."

Chapter Nine
Cacophony

Brishelle woke up on Saturday morning without feeling as depressed as she had felt lately. For the past few days, she had been having trouble getting out of bed. She was relieved that her mother, although disappointed, was supportive of her having a baby. Brishelle didn't tell her mom that the thought of having an abortion crossed her mind. Her mother encouraged her to keep and raise the child, despite the circumstances. However, Brishelle was still deathly afraid to tell AJ that she was having his child.

She knew AJ might not react by jumping for joy, but she knew he would eventually support her. This wasn't how she pictured she and AJ having their first child, but she thought that maybe this was the first step toward creating a family with him. She wondered if Tasha couldn't have children and that was why they still didn't have any. She knew he would be incredibly excited to have a son as all men were. She also knew that men were weak for their little princess daughters, too.

She decided that she would stay away from the church while she was pregnant. She might visit every once in a while as the child grew up. She planned to join another church in the meantime. She wanted to go to the largest church in the Los Angeles area, which was a megachurch. If she was there, no one would know much about her and wouldn't ask her too many questions.

Brishelle had a tiny apartment that wouldn't be the best environment to raise a child in the long run, but she vowed to make it work. All her money would have to go to formula, diapers, and buying a crib for now. She hoped her baby shower would relieve her of buying most of the small stuff like clothes. She needed even more money to raise the child, though, and wondered if she should quit the online magazine altogether and get a higher paying salaried job in either digital media or advertising. She had no idea if AJ would support her enough financially. However, she did plan to sue for child support when she proved the baby was his.

Her mother was clearly upset that she had lied to her the last time they spoke on the phone, but Brishelle figured she would get over it, eventually.

Brishelle decided that it was finally time to call her best friend and tell her about everything. She and Tiera were like sisters, and she couldn't handle keeping this nightmare of hers a secret forever.

Brishelle unblocked her number and called her.

"Hello, Tiera?"

"Brishelle? Oh, I see you been ignoring me and everything."

"No, I just been going through some things, girl. It's been crazy."

"So, you've been going through some things and decide to block me?" Tiera questioned.

"It's not like that, Tiera. I just didn't wanna talk to anybody. I didn't want to talk to my own mother for a while, but I ended up calling her recently."

"So, something must have happened. How much money you need?"

"I don't need any money, Tiera. I just need you to be supportive."

"Supportive about what?"

"I'm about to tell you. So…I'm pregnant."

"What? By who?"

"Girl, I don't know if I should tell you. You'll go off on me."

"Brishelle…you might as well tell me now because I'ma find out and get mad anyway."

"So…I'm pregnant by someone at church."

"Who? The pastor?"

"No, Tiera! The keyboard player."

"Girl, no! Not the one who's married!"

"Yes…we were messing around, and now I'm having his baby."

Tiera must have sat in silence for about thirty seconds before she was finally able to speak.

"Brishelle, you were messing around with a married man? What did your mother say?"

"She was pissed off," Brishelle sighed.

"Well, I'm pissed off, too. I thought you were better than this, Bri."

"I know, Tiera. I'm ashamed of myself, you don't have to make it worse."

"Well, I didn't know you were that fuckin' desperate that you would not only sleep with somebody's husband, but then turn around and get pregnant."

Brishelle started to cry. Her best friend being disappointed in her hurt her the most. She didn't know how she could redeem herself after this.

"So, are you keeping it, Bri?"

"Yeah…I am."

"Have you told him?"

"No, not yet."

"Well, when you gonna tell him?"

"I was gonna tell him in person, but I don't know when. I'm sure he has my number blocked because I tried calling him and texting him and it wouldn't go through."

"Bri…you gonna break that man's family up. This is crazy. You not ready for a kid your-damn-self."

"I know…but I'll make it work. My parents are gonna help me, and then I'll probably get some child support from AJ."

"Now, Bri…you know he's not gonna claim that baby."

Brishelle sat and thought. She wanted to make this all go away, but she just couldn't see herself taking a baby's life or sending them out to be adopted.

"I'm going to raise my child, and I'm going to get a DNA test."

"What, on *Maury*?" Tiera seemed exasperated.

"No, he's the only man I've been with. I'm sure I'm the only woman he was messing around with."

"And how do you know this, Bri? I know some people who know AJ from college, and he was one of the biggest hoes on campus."

Brishelle's heart sank. She hadn't really asked anyone else about AJ's track record. She had been so enamored by his looks. She wished she could have asked

Tiera some more information about him before she got too caught up.

"See, now, I would've told you some real tea I got on him, but you acted like you didn't wanna talk to me anymore. I almost guarantee you not the only woman he was messing around with."

"Well, OK, Tiera. Whatever. I'm pregnant now, and he's the daddy, so I'm gonna have to move forward with my life."

"You put yourself through some major bullshit. I mean, I'll support you, but if I were you, I'd lay low for a while."

"What do you think I'm doing, Tiera?"

"I'll call you back, Brishelle."

Brishelle knew that whenever Tiera called her by her first name, she was through with her. She hoped their friendship could survive this. Brishelle didn't understand why her friend was so angry with her. She was acting like

237

she was pregnant by *her* man. Brishelle concluded that at least she was pregnant by a successful real estate agent who was talented in music. She thought that at least her child would come out intelligent.

She went over to her mother's house to finally have a sit-down discussion about how they would move forward with this baby. Her mother talked to her about finances, childcare, and AJ's potential contribution. Brishelle was overwhelmed with how she would take care of this baby. Thoughts of having an abortion kept resurfacing in her mind. She really wasn't sure if AJ would step up and be a father, but a piece of her wanted to hold out hope that he would.

Part of her hoped that this baby would bring them back together and he would finally want to start a family with her. She thought that he was the type of man who wouldn't abandon his child and would do his best to make sure they were well taken care of. Once most of the shock went away, she expected him to step up and take care of his responsibilities.

Brishelle asked her mother if she could contact AJ through her phone. She said AJ wasn't picking up any of her calls or answering her texts anymore. Her mother told her she could.

She hadn't seen so much worry on her mother's face before. Her mother's hair had gone grayer, and she looked more worn out than she remembered. She hated that she would have to put her mother through the stress of helping raise her own grandchild. Her father was always drunk or out drinking with the men in front of the liquor store, so she knew it would just be up to her and her mother to care for this baby.

Brishelle sent a text to AJ.

Hey, AJ, this is Brishelle. My phone stopped working, so I thought I'd contact you.

He didn't respond for another ten minutes.

She suddenly saw the three dots blinking on her mother's iPhone and began to fear the worst.

Yeah…what's up?

Oh…um…I just hadn't talked to you in a while and I really wanted to talk to you about something important, so I was wondering if we could meet up very soon.

I don't know about anytime soon. I been real busy. What's wrong? Just tell me.

Brishelle replied quickly.

It's just not a conversation to have on my mother's phone. Plus, I noticed you don't pick up my calls or texts anyway.

Oh yeah…I did block you lol. But I can unblock you right now if you wanna talk business. I mean, I don't know what you want. I'm not trying to be in a relationship right now if that's what you wanted.

No, that's not it, but I do want to talk to you soon. Can I call you tonight, so we can set up a meeting?

A meeting? You tryna give me some money? LOL.

No, nigga. It's important, so it needs to be a face to face conversation.

Yeah, a'ight. You can't call me until after 9, but you can text me in a few minutes though. I'm at work.

OK.

Brishelle deleted the text thread as soon as she sent her last text.

"What was all that about?" Her mother looked at her with a mixture of anger and confusion.

"It wasn't anything."

"Must have been something, Breezy. What that man say?"

"He just said he would talk to me later because he's at work."

Her mother gave her the 'I don't believe you' look and rolled her neck. She was busy cutting up vegetables to put in her salad. Her mother was always on some temporary health kick.

"Here...eat some of this salad when I get through. You need to start getting healthy for the baby."

"I'm OK, momma. I'm not that hungry. I'll eat later."

Brishelle began to feel depressed once again. She had suddenly lost her appetite after the reality hit that there was a possibility that AJ wouldn't be as involved in his child's life as she thought.

"I just never pictured myself as a baby momma," Brishelle said in an almost muffled voice to her mother.

"Nobody told you to open your legs to a married man. You knew that man was married! It's not like he was lying to you. You also knew how to use protection because I know I taught you that. You're thirty-two years old. You're too old to be making mistakes like this."

"OK, momma, damn!"

"Don't you cuss at me, gal!"

"I'm not cussing, I'm just saying that what's done is done, and I can't do anything about it. Do you want me to have an abortion?"

"I didn't say all that, Breezy. I want the best for this child, but you have to understand that the consequences of your actions might be that man not being there for you."

"Well, AJ isn't like that. He's a family man."

"Yeah, to *his* family," her mother interrupted.

Brishelle was done talking to her mother about the situation and left.

"All right, momma. I guess I'll talk to you later."

"Yeah, well, you sure will talk to me later. I'm gonna be halfway responsible because children are not cheap."

Brishelle turned to walk out of the doorway. She would save her tears for when she got home. She hated crying in front of her mother. Her mother rarely comforted her when she cried when she was younger. She lacked emotion when it came to sensitive topics and would rather rant about it. She was never the touchy-feely-make-you-feel-better mother.

She hoped she would change once she saw her grandchild. Brishelle hoped she'd be a much more loving mother than her mother ever was.

Brishelle drove off in her car, but instead of going home, she went to the mall. She walked in and found a store that sold maternity clothes. She wasn't showing enough to buy any at the moment, but she was interested in looking at some of the styles she would like to wear. She wanted to make entering motherhood a lot more real for her. She wanted to feel like a normal mother. She wanted to bask in the glow of being a pregnant mother, waiting for her bundle of joy to arrive.

She walked into another store that sold baby clothes and toys. She didn't know whether she'd be having a boy or girl, but she picked up a few items such as cute bibs and bottles she saw. She also purchased a few gender-neutral onesies. She thought it was never too early to start shopping for the baby.

She then looked at how much a nice crib and car seat cost and was instantly overwhelmed. She had never priced diapers and formula before, but she didn't understand why baby formula cost between twenty-five and forty dollars a pop. She was definitely going to need two paychecks to cover most of the expenses. She hadn't even thought about childcare because her mother was still working. She worked from home most of the time, but she also had to travel often and attend meetings.

She knew her career would never be the same, but she wouldn't rest until AJ also made some drastic changes in his daily routine since this was also his child.

After Brishelle purchased a few items, she headed back home to get some rest. She had begun to feel more tired than usual lately. She wasn't able to be as productive online for the past week. Her job had unfortunately become secondary to her personal life. She was starting to lose money, too. She had only made seventy-five percent of what she had made last year in advertising.

Brishelle texted AJ.

Hey, you busy?

He didn't respond. He also didn't read the text since he had his read receipts turned on.

She tried to keep her eyes open as she drove the five miles West, back home.

Brishelle took a nap for about forty-five minutes. She had never felt so tired in her life. When she woke up, she looked for the text from AJ, but he had yet to respond. She thought he was playing games again.

Brishelle did want to finally confront his wife Tasha about her relationship with AJ. She felt that it was the right thing to do and that she needed to come clean. She was tired of living in secret. She wasn't sure of when she'd do it. She remembered that she had her number saved from the choir group text.

She was also sure that she wanted to officially quit the choir. She thought she should text or call him to let him know. He had been nice to her before, so she didn't want to burn that bridge. Brishelle then received a call from a number she didn't recognize, but she knew the area code. She wondered if AJ was calling her from a different number.

"Hello?"

"Yes, is this Brishelle? This is Bishop Loving."

"Hello, Bishop, how are you?"

"Oh, I'm blessed! I just hadn't seen you in a while. My wife and I sure do miss your voice in the choir."

"Well, thank you, Bishop. I've been having some family problems that I've been dealing with, so I haven't been able to make it to church as often."

"Well, do you need some prayer, baby?"

"Yes, sir, I do."

Bishop Loving asked her to bow her head, and they both closed their eyes. Brishelle's phone was on speaker.

"Lord, I come to You today to ask You to bind whatever evil has come into this child's life. You know Your child, Lord, and I ask You to bless her. Please, Lord, whatever issues have come into her family, I ask You to bind it. My God is all powerful, and I know You can bring her out of whatever she is going through. Lord, I thank You for her deliverance in advance. You are worthy to be praised. Devil, get your hands off this child! You have no place here! I command you to loose from her life. In Jesus' mighty name I pray. Amen!"

Tears streamed down Brishelle's cheeks. She hadn't heard such a strong prayer meant for her personally in years. She felt instant shame for what she had done. She felt it more than she ever had since finding out she was pregnant. She truly admired Bishop Loving, and she felt terrible that she had let him down.

"Bishop, I know you're disappointed with me. I'm sure you've heard some things."

"What things? No, Brishelle, I ain't heard nothing. I just noticed that you haven't been coming and I got worried."

"I'm sorry, Bishop. I just haven't been feeling my best."

"Well, baby, church is the hospital. You come there to encourage your spirit. Don't turn your back on God."

"Yes, sir, I know."

"All right, well, I hope to see you very soon. Be blessed."

"Thank you, Bishop, and thank you for calling."

Brishelle felt relieved that Bishop Loving didn't know anything about the affair. She guessed that it was just something the young people knew at church. Most of the church was full of old people with one foot in the grave anyway.

Brishelle decided to work up the courage to call Tasha, but she decided she would text her instead. AJ still hadn't texted her back, so she assumed he wouldn't do it at all.

Brishelle found Tasha's number in the group chat and texted her.

Hello, Tasha…this is Brishelle. I know you don't talk to me that often, but I thought it was important for me to come to you as a woman. I have been turning my life around, so what I'm about to say is not what's currently going on at all. AJ and I had a relationship going for a few months. I regret it now, but it happened, and I wanted to tell you that I'm sorry and I hope you can forgive me.

Brishelle sent the text and breathed deeply to calm herself down. Her heart wouldn't stop beating ferociously.

She saw that Tasha also had her read receipts on.

She read it but didn't respond for another twenty minutes.

So...I knew this already. However, the devil is a lie if you think you gonna break up my family. Just in case you didn't know...we're expecting a child. I ask that you give us space and privacy. If not, you will have to deal with the consequences. I do not want to have to bring a restraining order against you. Please stay away from our family. I hope for the best. Thank you.

Brishelle was startled by her response. She was shocked that she had forgiven AJ and decided to start a family with him. Brishelle was not only pregnant, but her child was going to have a brother or sister. She wondered what these "consequences" were, but she decided it was best to not text her back. Tiera told her that AJ had been sleeping around since college, and she knew that AJ and

Tasha had been together since college. She figured she must be used to him sleeping around.

Brishelle then received a random text from someone she didn't know.

So, you're the bitch who's been sleeping with AJ. This isn't Tasha, I'm her best friend. She told me you texted her. I know you gonna block me, but I just wanna let you know that if we ever see you around here, we will fuck you up. Trust. Tasha is a sweet girl, but I'm not. I ain't never been scared to beat a bitch ass. You a nasty-ass hoe. Fuck you. That's on everything.

Brishelle sat there confused and afraid. She didn't know what to do. She thought about just raising the baby on her own and cutting AJ off completely, but she didn't want her child to grow up without a father. She had a father, but he was always drinking. She felt like he was not as present in her life as he could have been

It was about 9:15 p.m., and she was beginning to nod off to the lull of the TV in the background. She turned it off and played some relaxing music on her phone to get her mind off of everything. Thoughts kept swirling around in her head. She didn't know what her next move should be. She felt bad that she was going to bring an innocent child into a situation like this.

Brishelle was tired, but she thought it would be best to give AJ a call now, so she could clear her mind. She called his number, and it rang several times. He didn't pick up. She called him again, and he still didn't pick up.

Brishelle laid face down on her bed and cried so intensely, her nose was stuffed up, and her pillow was almost drenched. Thoughts of taking her own life and getting away from it all crossed her mind. She didn't know how she'd ever make it through what she had done to herself.

She knew no one trusted her now, and it was only a matter of time before she had no friends and family she could count on.

She drifted off to sleep, trying to erase the negative thoughts from her mind, but was unsuccessful. She eventually drifted off into a deep sleep.

Brishelle's phone rang in the middle of the night. It startled her. Phone calls in the middle of the night always meant that some man was trying to hook up with her, or someone had died.

"Hey, what's up?"

It was AJ.

"Hey…what you calling me so late for?"

"It's not *that* late, Grandma," AJ laughed.

Brishelle felt a little relieved that AJ was joking with her. She didn't want to start their conversation on a bad note.

"I just wanted to see you," he said.

"Can you see me now?"

"No…it's late. I can't see you right this minute."

Brishelle was extremely tired, but she was trying to keep her eyes open.

"Why can't you meet me during the day, so we can talk about this."

"Talk about what?"

AJ seemed to be getting more frustrated.

"Talk about what I want to talk about because I need to do it in person."

"OK, well, you can meet me on my lunch break tomorrow. We can meet at Denny's or something."

Brishelle rolled her eyes.

"Damn, nigga. From Beverly Hills Steakhouse to Denny's. It's like that?" Brishelle said jokingly.

"Well, damn, Miss Spoiled Ass. All right, Brishelle, we can meet up at that white boy hipster *Greene Café*."

Brishelle smiled. Part of her still wanted him, but she was trying to get rid of that feeling the best she could.

His voice, the rhythm of how he spoke each word, his breathing on the phone, all turned her on. He was like some type of poison with a sweet, addictive taste. Any and every drop could potentially kill her, but she kept taking sips.

"I'll meet you tomorrow at *Greene Café* then. I'll find the address. Is that near your job?"

"Yeah, the twenty-somethings go over there all the time. I don't be eating salads like that, but I'm still healthy, though."

Brishelle laughed.

"What time?"

"We can meet around noon to eat some dry-ass salad," he said.

She was kind of suspicious of him being in such a good mood because she was sure his wife had been cursing him out about their previous rendezvous.

"All right then, I'll see you soon then…bae."

She took her chance with calling him "bae" and regretted it immediately.

"All right, bye," he said.

He hung up the phone abruptly. She wondered if he had even heard her.

Brishelle fell back asleep, but this time, on her stomach.

She'd have to get used to it for the next few months.

In the daytime, Brishelle felt a lot better than most mornings. She didn't feel as queasy and was able to get on her computer and work on a few things. She had multiple freelance writers working on the magazine now. She just wasn't able to keep up the day-to-day writing like she used to. She mainly maintained the website and made sure that her advertisers were pleased.

When it got closer to noon, Brishelle dressed in a simple t-shirt and jeans with a black pea coat since it was a little cool outside. She hadn't felt her best lately, but she didn't want to make that too obvious to AJ. She wore her hair down and let it swing down to the middle of her back. She wore a little more makeup than usual, a shirt that fit her loosely and stretchy skinny jeans. She left the top button open since her clothes were starting to get tighter and she didn't feel like buying new ones just yet. She hoped she hadn't gained too much noticeable weight.

Brishelle arrived at the *Green Café* around 11:50 and looked around to see if she saw AJ. She didn't, so she decided to have a seat near the bar area to wait for him. She pretended to be engrossed in her phone so she wouldn't sit around, looking awkward while she waited for him.

She was about to text him to see where he was, but she saw him walk from the parking lot to the entrance of the cafe. It was a mostly white and hipster establishment, so AJ stuck out like a sore thumb.

He had a buttoned shirt on and slacks. Before he came in, it seemed like he had forgotten to remove something from his shirt, and he turned back around. Brishelle thought it was strange, but she thought nothing more of it.

He walked back inside and looked around to see if he saw Brishelle, and she immediately caught his eye. He smiled and made his way over to the bar section.

"You didn't eat already?" he said as he gave her one of those church hugs.

"No, I was waiting for you."

"OK, well, let's go order. What they got besides salad?"

Brishelle smiled. She missed at least having him as a friend. She knew that once she hit him with this baby bombshell, it was only a matter of time before they were at odds with one another again. She hoped for the best.

They ordered two Chinese chicken salads, and he paid for both. She ordered a lemonade, and he ordered iced tea. The two sat down in a booth, sitting across from one another. There was a pause of awkward silence, then AJ cut in.

"So…what did you bring me here to tell me?"

Brishelle took a deep breath and looked at AJ in his midnight-colored eyes.

"I'm…" She paused.

"You're what, Brishelle?"

"I'm…pregnant, AJ. It's yours."

The server brought their plates of salad and drinks. They both immediately lost their appetite.

"Wait, what? You trippin'. I mean, like, fuck, man. I'm 'bout to have a baby with my wife, I can't do this."

"What do you mean, you can't do this?" Brishelle interrupted.

"Like, I mean, how you know it's mine? I'm the only nigga you been with?"

"The fuck!" Brishelle almost yelled. "Are you serious right now?"

"Man, my wife been trippin' like crazy lately. She knows about us, and now she thinks I'm trying to leave her and I'm not."

"No, you're not," Brishelle said swiftly, "but you are gonna help me take care of this child."

"I mean, I can…if it's mine."

"You really believe this baby is not yours? You are the only nigga I been with!"

A few of the restaurant patrons turned their heads.

"Will you stop being so loud? Everybody and their momma can hear us."

"I don't care who hears that you're an ain't shit nigga!" Brishelle said in a loud whisper.

"Wow, OK, Brishelle. This is just a way for you to get me back in your life and it's not gonna work. I have a family now, and I'm not trying to leave my wife. You knew there was a chance all this wasn't gonna work out."

Brishelle tried to keep the tears from forming in her eyes. She didn't want to cry. Her mother told her to never cry in front of a man because they didn't react to emotions the same way women do.

"Why are you doing this to me, AJ?"

"Doing what to you? I don't need this. I don't need another baby, and I know I can't be the only one you were fuckin' around with. I mean, I know we fucked, too, but damn…"

"AJ, I'm just done. You think I'm trying to get money out of you, but all I need is help for this child that *we* created."

"Look, Brishelle."

"No, look, AJ! Once this child is born, I will demand a DNA test. You are not getting out of this shit. You'll just have two kids now."

"Do what you want, I guess. Look, I gotta go. I only gotta hour lunch and I need to start heading back because this place is kinda far."

"Bye, AJ."

He stood up from the table without having touched his food.

Brishelle sat and cried uncontrollably at the table. Snot filled her nose, and her eyes were bright red. The white, female server came by and rubbed her back and gave Brishelle some tissue to blow her nose.

"Yeah, honey, he's not worth it. He looks like such a douche."

Chapter Ten
Rebirth

"If it's a boy, I think I'm gonna name him Alexander Temple." Brishelle was lying down on her mother's couch, midday Saturday.

"You not gonna give the child his daddy's name?" her mother questioned.

"Well, I mean, he says he doesn't believe he's the father, so I might not have any choice but to give the baby my name."

"Well, then, that's a doggone shame."

"Momma, look, it's gonna be OK. I don't need him anyway."

Brishelle felt defeated, but she didn't want to let her mother see her in such a state of weakness.

"You need to get a DNA test and sue for child support. If this baby is his, he don't need to skip out on his responsibilities.

"I know, momma. I want him to be part of my child's life, but if he doesn't, then that's him. I can be my child's mother and father. I don't need him."

Her mother looked at her sternly.

"Brishelle…now, maybe I told you that you could be anything you wanted to be when you were little, but baby, you can't take the place of no man. If he don't step up like he should, then you need to get back right with God and let Him help you raise this child. Every woman needs help. You can't be no man, and if you have a boy, you sho won't be able to teach him how to be a man."

"I know, but I'm just saying that if he doesn't want to be in the picture."

"Brishelle…this was your fault. You set that child up for failure by opening your legs to an unavailable man. You *knew* there was a possibility that this man wouldn't be around, and you still had a baby by him."

"So…do you want me to abort the child?" Brishelle said sarcastically.

"I didn't say all that. God loves all His children, but God also hates sin, and He can't bless you when you're sinful."

"So, my baby is not a blessing?"

"It is, Brishelle, but the sin was wrong, and you ought to learn from it! That man don't want no family with you. You must have thought that having a baby by him would make him want to leave his wife and be with you."

"No, I didn't, momma! You bring God up in every conversation. I'm not trying to have church right now. I'm pregnant, and I'm trying to do my best. The baby just happened. I was not trying to get pregnant by that man on purpose, so you got me all wrong."

"You should have had better sense then."

"Well, momma, maybe you should have had better sense than to marry some alcoholic who barely took care of us when I was younger. My brother don't even come around no more because of the crap he put us through. How about that?"

"Now, Brishelle! How dare you bring up my business to compare to you having this illegitimate baby. I ain't never had no illegitimate kids by no man. Your father wasn't drinking when I met him. That started after he lost his job, so speak what you know. He was a good father to you. Who put you in private school? Who took you to those dances? Who took you to college to settle in your dorm room? Had that man fixing up all kinds of gadgets you don't use now…for you!"

Brishelle started to get infuriated. She hated arguing, and she especially hated arguing with her mother. Her mother was one of the last people left who she could count on in her life. Everyone else had turned their back on her.

"He only did those things because you fussed at him! He was not a good father, and I still remember those times he put his hands on you! AJ may have been married, but he wasn't no abuser. I know better!"

"Get your behind out my house! You ol' ungrateful jezebel of a woman. I raised a complete disgrace. May God have mercy on you! Figure out how to take care of that baby your-doggone-self! Up here treating me like I'm the one halfway responsible for that ol' illegitimate child you got."

Brishelle stormed out of her mother's apartment and back to her car. She was almost about to curse her mother out, but she stopped herself. She officially had no one on her side, and since AJ was acting "brand new," she couldn't trust him anymore.

She went home and buried herself in her work once again to get her mind off everything. Every ten minutes or so, she would drift back into worrying about AJ and that unknown number that threatened her. She wondered if she should buy a gun just in case, so she could protect herself and her baby. She didn't fear AJ, but his wife seemed like she had some hoodrat friends who would try and find out where she lived.

Brishelle decided to shift her attention more towards motherhood. She thought she would definitely be able to care for the baby herself for now. She had saved up money for emergencies, but eventually, she might need a side hustle to keep the bills paid. She wasn't letting AJ off the hook just yet. She was definitely going to do a DNA test when the baby was born and sue him out his pants.

She had no contact with family or friends anymore, and that scared her. This one mistake of a relationship had cost her, and she didn't think she'd be able to pay her debt anytime soon.

She tried to keep herself busy for the time being and do some more shopping with the baby. She had been keeping a low profile by going to malls and shopping centers that were outside of her area, but this time, she decided to stay local.

The Western Pavilion mall was crowded on a Friday afternoon. Brishelle could barely find parking. She finally parked at almost the furthest spot she could find. She almost snagged her ring on her clothes as she got out of the car. She had been wearing a cubic zirconia ring on her left ring finger lately. She thought it would make people ask fewer questions. She didn't want to be lumped with the ghetto baby mommas. She thought she was much classier and more educated than these hood boogers running around.

She headed to the baby section of a department store. She remembered she had a hundred-dollar gift card from her mother that she had never spent. She thought she would have to start spending everything on the baby now. She assumed she wouldn't be able to buy for herself for a long time. She was OK with that. She wanted to give her baby everything she never had.

While walking out of the department store, Brishelle couldn't believe her eyes. She saw AJ's wife Tasha walking with a friend through the mall. She saw her enter a maternity store and thought she should have never tried to hit up the local mall. She usually always ran into someone she knew.

Brishelle decided to walk the other way and hoped she wouldn't see her. She began to leave the mall, but then felt she shouldn't have to be afraid of anyone. She was willing to protect herself and her baby at all costs.

She went toward the dining cafeteria and stood in line to get Chinese food. She paid for her food and took her tray to sit down.

Tasha and her friend passed right by her. They didn't see her. Brishelle wondered if that was the friend who had sent the anonymous text message.

Suddenly, Tasha turned around and made eye contact with Brishelle. She told her friend what she saw, and they both turned around. The friend sneered at Brishelle and was about to come towards her. Brishelle's stomach suddenly felt upset.

Tasha tried to pull her away, but the woman got away from her and stormed toward Brishelle.

"So, you're the bitch who's been sleeping with my best friend's husband!"

The cafeteria became so silent, you could have heard a pin drop. Even babies stopped crying, and a few of the cashiers temporarily paused.

Brishelle stood up from her seat and said, "Yes, bitch, I am. What the fuck are you gonna do about it?"

Tasha swiftly ran over to where her best friend was.

This was the first time Brishelle and Tasha looked at each other, eye to eye.

"I'm not with him anymore. We broke up. He's all yours," Brishelle said.

"Bitch, if this wasn't a public place, I'd swing at your ass. I also got to protect my unborn child."

"Well, guess what? I have to protect my unborn child, too."

The patrons who were eating in the cafeteria had their eyes wide open and were dead silent.

No one moved.

"Tasha, let's go. Let's leave this bitch alone. I'll knock her ass out for you."

"Do it, bitch!" Brishelle yelled.

Tasha's friend took her fist and swung it at Brishelle's face. Brishelle moved back quickly and ran. She grabbed her bag and ran so fast, she almost slipped.

She didn't want mall security to get involved. She didn't feel like being pregnant and in jail.

She drove back home, embarrassed, scared, and dismal. Her head was spinning with the amount of problems she had put herself through. She had to pull over and get herself together before she drove back home.

All she wanted was to finally meet the love of her life, and now she was in a mess that she would never be able to get herself out of. She seriously thought of moving out of the state and going to live in a rural area where all the redneck white people lived.

She decided to text her ex-boyfriend from college. He was one of the last men she had loved, even though she didn't consider herself to have ever been in love with him. They had broken up on good terms. He had gotten a job in another city, and they had grown apart.

She texted him to see how he was doing. She just wanted to talk to someone who wouldn't judge her and had no idea what was going on in her life.

He texted her back.

Brishelle? Damn, it's been minute. How have you been?

I'm good, Carl. I've just been living life.

What you been up to?

Oh, nothing…I just wanted to talk. We used to be so close once, even after we broke up.

Yeah, we were, Brishelle.

He didn't text her back as quickly as she wanted, so she decided to still try and make conversation.

So...when you gonna be back in L.A.?

Not anytime soon, he replied. *Why do you ask?*

Oh, nothing. I just miss you.

Brishelle, I'm not trying to get back in a relationship right now or date. I'm kind of busy with life at the moment. I just got promoted, but we can still be text buddies when I'm not busy.

Oh, no...I wasn't thinking of dating. I just missed talking to you. You were funny and everything.

Yeah, you were funny, too, Brishelle. But it was nice talking to you, though. I got to get back to work. I'll hit you up later.

Brishelle felt dumb and awkward. This was her last chance to talk to a man who had at least cared about her.

She remembered they had broken up because of his job, but Brishelle remembered not caring that much because physically, he just wasn't her type. He was more of a "nice guy," or more like a brother. She thought he would have been the perfect father and husband. She wished she wasn't so shallow.

Brishelle drove home and decided to take a nap. She was exhausted.

When she woke up, she texted AJ once again. She wanted him to know that she wanted to be back on good terms and wondered if they could be friends for the baby. She clearly stated that she did not want a relationship and that she respected his marriage.

He did not respond but had read the text.

She was heated. She hated being left on read, especially by a man who didn't want to take care of his responsibilities.

Brishelle got in her car and headed toward his house. She made sure she put her gun in her car just in case someone tried to ambush her in their neighborhood. She knew Tasha's people probably knew what her car looked like by now.

It was raining heavily that day, and she felt her car slip on the road a few times. She began driving slower. She could barely see what was in front of her. She passed by at least two accidents on the freeway.

He lived in a suburb right on the outskirts of the city where few Black people lived, so she knew that if anyone saw her car, they would immediately know it was her. She slowly entered his neighborhood. He lived on a cul-de-sac, and most of the lights were on in the neighborhood. She had trouble finding his house at first because they all looked alike. She remembered that his house had a walkway that had lights on both sides and a bright red door.

The rain began to subside. Brishelle looked for his car and saw it parked in the driveway. However, she also saw the choir director Brandon's car parked behind his. Brishelle thought that was odd, but she figured that they were having a meeting.

Brishelle quickly walked up to the doorstep. She heard loud moans coming from the bedroom window.

She remembered AJ joking that he had spare keys under the welcome mat and could do that because he lived in a white neighborhood. She knew he must have told her that because he would have never fathomed Brishelle breaking into his house.

She truly wanted to know what those moans were. She was already intensely jealous of the woman he was having sex with. She remembered when those moans used to belong to her. He used to make her feel like she was the only woman who mattered in the whole world, and now he had completely ignored her as if she didn't exist.

She unlocked the door and put the key underneath the mat. She walked inside, and the moans got even louder. She saw two jackets sprawled on the couch, and the TV was left on.

Brishelle walked upstairs and went toward the door that was slightly open. She remembered that was where his bedroom was. She slowly opened the door in anticipation, and AJ was behind Brandon, pushing his penis into his butt as he moaned in ecstasy.

AJ had his eyes closed, and Brandon was biting a pillow, but she instantly knew it was him.
Brishelle was so shocked, she was at a loss for words.

"AJ?" Brishelle finally found the words to speak.

"Brishelle! What the fuck are you doing in my house!"

"I'm here because you're a bitch-ass nigga who wants to skip out on your responsibilities but sit up here and fuck dudes all day. What the fuck! You're gay?"

"Brishelle! On God! I swear yo' muthafuckin' ass better get the fuck out my house."

"How about you finish fucking Brandon's mothafuckin' ass. It looked like he was enjoying it!"

"OK, so…I have to leave. This is some crazy shit."

Brandon tried to find his underwear and pants that had been strewn all over the floor. He barely looked at Brishelle in the eyes.

"So, this is the choir director for Glory Harvest?" Brishelle said. "What a damn shame."

"Bitch, you knew I was gay. Prettier than your synthetic weave wearing ass. AJ was always fucking with me. I'd go get checked if I were you."

Brishelle's heart sank to her stomach. Not only was she pregnant, but she might also have an incurable disease because of her negligence to use protection.

AJ had his head down in his hands. He put his clothes on and stormed over to Brishelle as if he was about to hit her.

"Nigga, I wish you would put your hands on me!" Brishelle shouted.

"I'm not that kinda nigga, but you about to push me there, you fuckin' stalker. Who I fuck is none of your business."

"So, are you gonna tell your wife that you were not only having sex with me, but with Brandon, too? I bet she'll be more than shocked. She'll finally drop your dog ass. You not even straight."

AJ picked Brishelle up out of the bedroom and threw her down the stairs. She slipped down at least ten stairs until she caught herself. He then threw a heavy book at her that had been laying on the table.

Brishelle thought about her gun in the car, but she quickly decided it wasn't worth it.

"I can really fuck you up right now, but I won't. I ought to go to the police, bitch," Brishelle said.

"Bitch, I want you to! I'll tell them you broke into my house."

AJ was right. She had technically broken in. All she could think about right now was if her unborn child was all right.

"You are the father of this fucking baby, AJ! Fuck!"

"Prove it, nasty-ass bitch! Brandon was way tighter than your loose pussy ass!"

If Brishelle were lighter skinned, she would have been red.

Her hands were sweating, and her voice shook.

"I'll tell everybody at church you're gay! Trust. They'll take your homo ass off everything, including that keyboard."

"Do it, bitch! I'll tell them you slept with everybody in the church, including some of the women. They'll believe me way before they believe you. You ain't shit in the church. I been coming there since I was a baby and never stopped. I'll get a restraining order against your ass, too, since you can't seem to leave me the fuck alone."

Brandon had put on his clothes, grabbed his jacket, and was heading out the door.

"Ugly bitch!" he said as he slammed the door.

"Faggot-ass nigga!" Brishelle screamed.

She picked herself off the floor with her hands and fled down the stairs. AJ came after her, and she ran out of the door. His overwhelming presence scared her, and she felt like she had to run for her life. She didn't know what he wanted to do. She thought she saw a shiny object in his hand. She ran to her car and found the gun under her seat. She locked the car doors, and he went back inside and locked his door.

She knew that he might call the police, so she drove off as quickly as she could. She had never driven so fast in her life. She ran past the stop sign and entered the freeway going about eighty mph. She finally met a red light when she got off the freeway. Her heart was beating so fast, she felt as if she had to catch her breath and pull over on the side of the road. She was afraid that AJ had told the police her license plate number.

She drove back home, feeling lightheaded, queasy, and nervous. She couldn't call anyone for help. Her mother and her best friend were officially done with her. She suddenly felt totally alone.

She was still extremely shocked that AJ had been bisexual all along. She never caught on to any signs that he and Brandon may have liked each other. She knew Tasha might not ever find out about Brandon because she was so fixated on her. She wanted to expose AJ and Brandon, but she hadn't taken any pictures, so she knew no one would ever believe her.

She was suddenly afraid that she might have a virus or some disease since AJ seemed to have been messing around with multiple people. She had heard about men on the down low, passing the HIV virus to women all the time. She decided that she would go to the clinic in the morning to get checked out. She was going to have to make an appointment anyway to see the doctor since she was about ten weeks along.

Brishelle went to bed that night and turned her phone off. She usually never turned her phone off.

She didn't sleep that well because she was still afraid that AJ would find her, or the police would come to her door, looking for her. She hadn't stolen anything, but he might have had security cameras.

She would never give up on her child having a father. She figured that he might have a change of heart once he saw how much the child looked like him.

In the morning, Brishelle decided to lie in bed much longer than usual. She was officially depressed. She wondered if she would need some kind of medication to get her back to a state of happiness once again. She had no desire to do her job, leave the house, and especially not to be a mother.

The baby was growing inside of her, but she felt very little attachment to it. She felt terrible that she was angry about having this baby. She knew that she only felt this way because she would be having the baby alone. Her dreams of a picture-perfect family were gone. Who would want her now? She was pregnant by a married, secretly bisexual abuser who had pushed her down the stairs.

The only thing keeping her from not having an abortion was the fear that the death of that child would be seared into her conscience forever. She didn't want to have to bear the burden of potentially breaking up a family and murdering an innocent life.

Brishelle fell to her knees in prayer and asked God for His forgiveness. She hoped He would carry her through this trying time. She said that she would do His will if He brought her out of this mess she had gotten herself in. She said she wanted to live a life more pleasing to Him and was ashamed of what she had done. She vowed to never do it again if He would help her care for this child.

Her money was running low. Fewer and fewer readers were visiting *HeyBlackGrl!* and she didn't have as many advertisers as she had a couple of months ago. She was no longer able to pay her freelance writers and lacked enough interesting material to keep her readers engaged. She decided to put her website on hiatus for now and apply for other jobs that were hiring in digital media. She took some odd freelance writing jobs for now. She also decided that she should start selling some of her old, designer clothes for money.

She was also going to apply for welfare benefits since she could prove that she wasn't working, and the father was no longer in the picture. She hoped that they could eventually find her new housing once the money ran out to pay her one-thousand-dollar rent.

She had become the type of woman she had always despised. She was a single mother with no job and an "ain't shit" baby daddy.

She had become her worst enemy.

She was still educated and beautiful, but she knew that finding a job in her field of digital communications would not be easy as most jobs in that area were very competitive.

She didn't have the energy or the desire to keep up her website anymore. At this point, she was too depressed to work at all.

She got a sudden phone call. It was Bishop Loving.

Her heart started beating quickly. She wondered if he had finally found out the truth.

"Brishelle? How you doing?"

Bishop Loving had a thick southern accent. He had grown up in rural Mississippi and had a very gentle southern charm about him.

"Oh, I'm fine, Bishop. I've just been busy lately."

"Now I don't know why, but God put it on my heart to give you a call. Has everything been all right?"

"Everything's been all right, sir. I've been fine," Brishelle said in a sullen voice.

"Now, you don't sound fine, baby. Now I'm gonna pray for you, but I want you to do one thing for me."

"Yes, Bishop?"

"I want you to join us Sunday morning. I'm not asking for no offering. I just want you to be there. You know this is your church. I remember back when you were a baby. You cried during your whole christening ceremony. I also christened your older brother. I know you belong in the church, baby. God hates sin, but He loves the sinners."

Tears began to roll down Brishelle's cheeks all at once. The stream of tears fell into her lap.

"Pastor… I-I just been going through a hard time. I've made too many mistakes, and now I don't know what to do."

"Baby, God forgives. He can forgive anything. You just got to remember that you are loved, and He has not forsaken you. You turn your back on God, but He never turns his back on you."

Brishelle began to cry audibly into the phone. She felt like a child who was crying heavily after being beaten with a belt. She couldn't stop herself.

"I'm so sorry, Bishop. It's just been so bad. My family and friends...I just don't know. I did it to myself."

"Baby, God is a forgiving God," Bishop Loving interrupted. "Now, I need you to pray with me over the phone and promise you'll see me on Sunday."

"I promise, Bishop."

"Oh, Heavenly Father, we come to You today to ask You to heal this child. Heal her from whatever has come into her life. This is Your child, Father, and I know You can make a way. There is not a mountain or valley that You cannot reach. You made this world, Father, and You know exactly how to heal Your child. She is calling out and asking You to bless her, Lord. We need a turnaround, Lord. We need a miracle today, Lord! I bind that devil in the name of Jesus. Loose here, Satan! You are not wanted here you ol' lying wonder! Hey! Hey! Hey!

Hondulashondamonda! Thank you, Jesus! And in your holy name, I pray. Amen!"

"Amen," Brishelle whispered.

"All right, baby. Well, I'll see you this Sunday if the Lord's will."

"I'll see you Sunday, Bishop."

Brishelle felt somewhat better after she hung up. She felt like she had one person who still believed in her even though her whole world was falling apart. However, Brishelle knew that it was only a matter of time before the pastor knew what she and AJ had been up to, and then that bridge would be burned as well.

She decided she would attend the service anyway. She wasn't showing too much, so she could wear a dress that hid most of her stomach.

On Sunday, she slowly got dressed for church. She wore her hair back and in a loose bun. She didn't feel like curling it or styling it. She wore a simple black dress that fit her loosely. She wore a gray blazer that covered most of her chest and stomach as well. She even wore stockings this time. She wore heels that weren't as tall as what she usually wore. She looked much more "sanctified" than she ever had in her life. She felt that if she was going to change her life, she was going to have to dress in the "holiness uniform" from now on.

Brishelle drove to the church, and she saw that the parking lot was almost full. She found a spot furthest from the front of the church so she wouldn't get blocked in.

Church had already started when she walked in. The praise team was leading the service. Tasha was in the middle of Kimiesha and Tyanna, who Brishelle used to sing with. Brishelle sat in the back corner of the church. She looked around to see if she saw AJ on an instrument. He was on the keyboard towards the side of the church, smiling and laughing with the drummer.

Tasha didn't seem to have noticed her. Brishelle decided she wouldn't stay that long, but she did want Bishop Loving to see that she had come to the service. She hoped that he wouldn't ask her to stand, or worse, sing.

As service went on, Bishop Loving asked AJ and Tasha to stand in the front of the altar as if he were marrying them. The two tightly held hands and looked at no one else but the Bishop.

There was no music playing, and the church was almost dead silent.

"Church! I want to add a special segment to today's service to rededicate this married couple to God."

Brishelle sat motionless with her eyes only slightly peering over the towering church hats in front of her.

She heard a woman next to her whisper to someone, "I heard she had a miscarriage."

Bishop Loving went on. "Saints! There are some devils in this here church and beyond its walls that want to tear down the foundation of a man married to his wife, but we're not gonna let that devil win. I am rededicating this couple to You, Lord, right now! God shall bless this union. What God has put together…"

"Let no man separate!" the church shouted in unison.

"Hallelujah," he went on. "Now, let us bow our heads in prayer."

AJ looked back towards the corner of the church where Brishelle was sitting and stared at her with a cold and bitter look in his eyes.

"It's not over, nigga," she mouthed as she stared back at him with a look that could scare the devil back to hell.

To Be Continued

Visit Us At
www.Urbanchapterspublications.com

CPSIA information can be obtained
at www.ICGtesting.com
Printed in the USA
LVHW041618020719
623003LV00015B/690/P